CALGARY PUBLIC LIBRARY

JAN   2017

DreamWorks Trolls © 2016 DreamWorks Animation LLC. All Rights Reserved.
Published in the United States by Random House Children's Books, a division
of Penguin Random House LLC, 1745 Broadway, New York, NY 10019, and
in Canada by Penguin Random House Canada Limited, Toronto, in conjunction
with DreamWorks Animation LLC. Random House and the colophon are
registered trademarks of Penguin Random House LLC.

randomhousekids.com

ISBN 978-0-399-55909-9 (hc) — ISBN 978-0-399-55910-5 (paperback)
ISBN 978-0-399-55911-2 (ebook)

Printed in the United States of America

10 9 8 7 6 5 4 3 2 1

Trolls

The Junior Novelization

Adapted by Dave Lewman

Random House 🏠 New York

CHAPTER
1

Once upon a time, in a happy forest filled with happy trees, there lived the happiest creatures the world has ever known: the Trolls!

They loved nothing more than to sing and dance and hug. And dance and hug and sing, and so on.

Things were going along pretty well until one day, all their singing and dancing attracted an unfortunate audience: a nasty brute known as a Bergen.

Bergens—towering giants compared with the tiny Trolls—were the most miserable creatures in all the land, in any direction you cared to go and as far as you could walk. Instead of hugs and songs, they gave each other kicks and wedgies and grimaces and growls. Whenever clouds appeared in the sky, they floated right above the Bergens and dropped cold rain on them. When the Bergens saw how happy the Trolls were, they longed to have some of that happiness for themselves.

Hearing the Trolls sing, one hungry Bergen wandered into the happy forest to find out where the melody was coming from. He saw a cheerful Troll climb out of a colorful pod hanging in a tree. The Troll walked onto a tree branch, opened his arms wide, and started to sing.

"*Oh, what a happy, happy day! The happiest day I ever—*"

The Bergen grabbed the Troll and popped him in his mouth! *GULP!* The giant beast swallowed the little Troll whole. The second the Troll hit his tummy, the Bergen experienced intense feelings he'd never felt before—*Joy! Delight! Bliss!*—each with an exclamation point. These were words he'd never used, but they seemed to describe the sensations he was having.

The other Trolls stared at the Bergen, horrified!

"Oh my gah!" said a girl Troll, her eyes round with terror.

CHAPTER 2

When the Bergen got home, he told his fellow Bergens about the amazing experience he'd had. At first they were confused.

"You mean," said one of them, "you found a new way of feeling miserable?"

"No," said the Bergen. "Not miserable. I felt . . ." He searched for the right word. He'd heard it a long time ago, but it was a word the Bergens almost never used. "Hap-p-py," he said slowly. "That's it. I felt happy!"

The other Bergens' beady eyes widened in wonder. "Show us!" one of them roared. The first Bergen led them all back to the Trolls' happy forest, running the whole way. The Bergens began snatching the mouth-sized Trolls out of the trees and gobbling them up. Delicious! Scrumptious! Why would the Bergens ever want to be anywhere else? This forest full of Trolls was the tastiest place in the world!

In no time at all, the Bergens had chopped down most of the trees in the woods to build Bergen Town, an ugly village surrounding the one remaining Troll Tree. They built a sturdy cage around the tree. The Trolls they hadn't eaten yet were trapped!

Eating the Trolls made the Bergens feel so happy, they started a tradition. Once a year, they gathered around the Troll Tree to taste happiness on a holiday they called Trollstice.

One particularly beautiful Trollstice morning, a young Bergen zoomed through the hallways of Bergen Town's royal castle on his bike. He wore a crown because he was Prince Gristle, the only son of King Gristle and heir to the Bergen throne.

Breathing hard, Prince Gristle rode his bike right up a stairway, through a door, and into his dad's bedroom. He jumped off the bike and onto his sleeping father's stomach. King Gristle stirred, and his crown slipped down over one of his eyes. He liked to wear his crown even when he slept so there was no chance of anyone ever, *ever*, EVER forgetting that he was ruler of the Bergens—top dog, A#1.

"Good morning, Daddy!" Prince Gristle sang. His father groaned and tried to shoo his son away, hoping for a few more minutes of sleep. But the prince was so excited that he burrowed under the sheets and scurried up and down the length of the big bed. "Daddy, wake up!" he shouted. "Daddy, wake up! Wake up! Wake up, Daddy!"

King Gristle kept snoring. *Zzzzz . . .*

Prince Gristle decided to try whispering. "Wake up, Daddy," he said softly. Then he tore open his father's nightshirt, grabbed a handful of his chest hair, and ripped it out. *"Wake up!"*

"YEOWCH!" King Gristle yelped.

Prince Gristle bounced on his dad's furry belly like it was a trampoline. "Daddy! Daddy! Daddy! Daddy! Daddy!"

"Gristle?" the king said, snatching his son in midair. "What time is it?"

"It's Trollstice!" Prince Gristle yelled, unable to control himself.

King Gristle smiled. Trollstice! Of course! He'd almost forgotten! The Bergens' only holiday!

After getting dressed and eating breakfast, the king threw open the doors to the castle. "Trollstice!" he exclaimed. "Our one day to be happy!" He set Prince Gristle on his shoulders.

As they headed toward the Troll Tree, the king and the prince could hear the Bergens all over town chanting, "Trolls! Trolls! Trolls! Trolls!"

When King Gristle approached the cage surrounding the Troll Tree, the guards stepped aside to let him through. The king lifted the prince off his shoulders and set him on the ground.

A team of chefs in military-style uniforms whipped out razor-sharp knives. They scraped their blades together, which sent sparks shooting toward two large hibachi grills. *WHOOSH!* A giant burst of flame leapt from each grill.

From the smoke a voice said, "Please give it up for your Keeper of the Trolls, your Minister of Happiness, your Royal Chef . . . ME!"

"Ooooh!" Prince Gristle said, impressed—and a little bit scared.

A shadowy, imposing figure strode through the dark smoke. . . .

CHAPTER 3

The Royal Chef. She was mean and miserable-looking, even for a Bergen.

She was in charge of cooking Trolls for the Bergens. Which meant she was in charge of their happiness. Which gave her power. And Chef *liked* power. A lot.

"CHEF! CHEF! CHEF!" the Bergens roared, cheering for their beloved cook. Chef stared at the crowd of Bergens until they fell silent, waiting for her to speak.

"This is a very special Trollstice," Chef announced, "as there is one amongst us who has never tasted a Troll."

Prince Gristle's face lit up. "Ooooh, me! She's talking about me!"

Chef stared down at the young Bergen. "Prince Gristle, the time has come."

The prince looked nervous. His proud father tied a brand-new Troll bib around his neck and gently urged him to step forward. Prince Gristle hesitated. "It's okay, son," King Gristle said reassuringly. "I was nervous when I had my first Troll, too."

"Okay," Prince Gristle said, trying to swallow his fear.

The king gave him a thumbs-up. "That's my boy!"

Chef leaned down and put her hand on Prince Gristle's shoulders. She looked him in the eye and said seriously, "It is my sacred duty to initiate you in the ways of true happiness."

Chef stood up straight and walked over to the gate in the cage around the Troll Tree. She took out a large ring of keys, selected one, and unlocked and opened the rusty gate. *CREEEEAK . . .*

All the Bergens in the crowd leaned forward, trying to catch a good view of the Troll Tree and its delicious inhabitants. Beautifully colored pods hung from its branches. "Oooooh," they murmured. "Trolls."

Unable to control himself, Prince Gristle ran past Chef and into the cage, staring up at the tree and the

Trolls on its branches. Chef followed him in, reached up, and plucked a Troll with a puff of pink hair off the tree. The prince tried to grab it, but Chef held it just out of his reach.

"I have chosen an extra-special Troll just for you," she said loudly, so everyone could hear. "The happiest, most positive, SWEETEST Troll of all. Because every prince deserves a princess, I present to you the one they call . . . Princess Poppy."

Prince Gristle impatiently jumped up and grabbed the pink-haired Troll from Chef.

He couldn't believe how lucky he was to *finally* have a Troll!

He was about to stuff the little Troll in his mouth but paused just long enough to whisper, "Please make me happy."

He bit down. *CRUNCH!* The Troll snapped in two. Prince Gristle chewed greedily. Then he looked puzzled and a little disgusted.

Beaming, Chef asked, "What are you feeling?"

The prince spat out a mouthful of wood bits. "This one's rotten!"

Chef grabbed the other half of the Troll out of Prince Gristle's hand and examined it closely. It wasn't a Troll at all! "It's fake!" she cried, horrified.

The Troll was, in fact, a clever decoy carved out of wood. Pink Troll hair had been glued to its head to fool the Bergens.

"FAKE?" the Bergens gasped, astonished. Nothing like this had ever happened in the history of Trollstice!

King Gristle rushed forward. "FAKE!" he roared, furious. *BAM!* The king kicked the trunk of the Troll Tree. Dozens of wooden Troll decoys fell from the branches and clattered to the ground.

"The Trolls are *gone*?" Prince Gristle wailed, deeply disappointed. How would he get his first taste of true happiness without a Troll to chomp on?

King Gristle wheeled around to face Chef, snarling. "WHERE ARE THE TROLLS?"

The Trolls were racing through the dark tunnels under the Troll Tree, following its winding system of long, gnarled roots. Old Trolls, young Trolls, boy Trolls, girl Trolls—all were running as fast as their little Troll legs could carry them. As they sprinted through the low dirt tunnels, their long hair streamed along the ceiling of the dark passageways.

"Go! Go!" shouted their leader, King Peppy. He stood in one of the tunnels, encouraging his fellow Trolls and holding a torch to light their way. They were passing an adorable, happy little Troll forward like a baton in a relay race. The pink-haired Troll was Princess Poppy, the very Troll Chef had planned to serve to Prince Gristle!

"We've got Poppy!" a guy Troll said, passing the baby princess along.

"Here comes Poppy!" a lady Troll said.

"We've got Poppy!" announced an old Troll.

"WHEEEEEEE!" Poppy cried, immensely enjoying her ride from Troll to Troll.

Finally, Princess Poppy was handed to her dad. "There's my princess!" King Peppy said.

"Da-da!" Princess Poppy burbled joyfully.

A kindly young Troll named Aspen hurried over to King Peppy. "Sir, some of the others can't keep up."

King Peppy tucked the pink-haired princess into his hair for safekeeping and rushed back into the darkness of the tunnel.

"No Troll left behind!" he called as he ran.

Soon the king spotted a mother Troll and her young child hesitating, not sure how to get past a puddle. King Peppy swept off his cloak and threw it over the puddle so the mother and her child could cross safely.

"Thank you, King Peppy!" the mother Troll said.

Running along the tunnel, his torch flickering in the darkness, King Peppy covered more puddles with pieces of his clothing. "Thank you, King Peppy!" cried a Troll named Cookie as she passed.

Shedding clothing as he went, the Trolls' leader was soon down to his tighty-whities. He stopped to lift a fallen root that was blocking the way. "Thank you, King Peppy!" said a Troll named Mandy. The king was about to turn around and start back when he heard an anguished voice calling from the darkness. "King Peppy!"

He sped to the side of Darius, a Troll who had fallen to the floor of the tunnel. "What is it, Darius?" the king asked anxiously.

"I can't go on," Darius said. "It's broken."

"What is?"

"My . . . spirit."

King Peppy put a reassuring hand on Darius's shoulder. "No, it's not."

Darius hesitated a moment, then smiled. "Thank

you, King Peppy!" he said. He stood up—and immediately collapsed to the ground again. "Ow!" he cried. "Oh, wait—no, it's not my spirit. It's my leg. It's definitely my leg."

King Peppy looked at Darius's leg, which was bent at a weird angle. Yep. It was broken. Without hesitating, the king bent and picked Darius up. He carried the injured Troll on his back. "No Troll left behind!" he repeated.

But as King Peppy made his way along the dark underground tunnel with Darius, pickaxes and shovel blades pierced the ceiling, threatening to collapse their escape route! *SHOONK! SHOONK! SHOONK!* King Peppy had to dodge the sharp blades as he ran through the passageway carrying his fellow Troll.

Aboveground, Chef's soldiers furiously stabbed the earth. They were determined to stop the Trolls.

"Daddy!" Prince Gristle cried. "Where are they? Where are the Trolls?"

King Gristle didn't know the answer. And not knowing made him even angrier. He turned to Chef. "Don't just stand there! Make my son *happy*!"

"He *will* be happy!" Chef insisted. She snatched a pickax from one of the soldiers and started stabbing the ground with it herself. *SHOONK!*

In the tunnel below, the pickax pierced the ceiling and snagged King Peppy's underwear! He was stuck!

At that point, King Peppy was carrying several other Trolls on his back in addition to Darius. He rolled them down the tunnel like bowling balls, straining to free himself. He did, and then— *SHWUNK!* The blade of a shovel slammed down in front of King Peppy, blocking his path and trapping him in the tunnel.

The tunnel led to an opening in the forest. The Trolls King Peppy had tossed now rolled out into the sunshine, collapsing at the feet of the other waiting Trolls.

"Where's King Peppy?" one Troll asked anxiously.

"I don't think he made it," Darius said sadly.

"Oh, no," said a little Troll. "Princess Poppy . . ."

But then they heard a voice. "When I say no Troll left behind, I mean"—King Peppy climbed out of the tunnel—"no Troll left behind!" He struck a heroic pose, holding Princess Poppy in one hand over his head. All the Trolls cheered, even though King Peppy was completely, utterly, stark naked.

"We all are safe," King Peppy announced. "But

we'll be a lot safer the farther we get from Bergen Town. Go, go! Hurry!"

The Trolls did not need to be told twice. They turned and ran away through the forest.

CHAPTER 4

In Bergen Town that night, King Gristle was not happy. In fact, he was even more miserable than usual. Trollstice had been ruined, his son was unhappy, and it was all Chef's fault.

"That's right! Take her away!" he shouted out a window of the castle. "Get her out of my sight!"

Below the window, a mob of angry Bergen townsfolk carried Chef through the streets, booing and jeering.

"She is hereby banished from Bergen Town!" the king proclaimed. "FOREVER!"

"Let go of me!" Chef told the furious Bergens, struggling to break free from their tight grips. "What do you think you're doing? Without me, who will be in charge of your happiness? Who will prepare the Trolls?"

"Thanks to you, there *are* no Trolls!" an angrier-than-angry Bergen snarled.

The mob dumped Chef outside the gates of Bergen Town. *SLAM!* The gates were shut. Chef got to her feet and called after the retreating mob, trying to sound humble. "Please! We can all be happy again! I'll find the Trolls. . . ."

But when the mob was gone, Chef let her hatred show—and it was not pretty. "And I'll shove them down your ungrateful throats," she grumbled. She turned and walked away, planning her revenge. She vowed to get back at the Bergens, no matter how long it took.

Back in the castle, Prince Gristle watched through a window as the mob carried Chef away. He walked sadly through the long Great Hall toward his father's throne, passing a young scullery maid named Bridget, who was mopping the floor. He found King Gristle on his throne with his chin in his hand, brooding.

"Daddy," the prince said, "I never got to eat a

Troll. What's gonna make me happy now?"

The king gently patted his knee. "Come here, son."

The prince climbed onto his father's knee. The king looked deeply into his son's big, hopeful eyes. "Nothing," he answered flatly. "Absolutely nothing. You will never, ever, ever, *ever* be happy."

"Never?" Prince Gristle asked in a small voice.

"Ever," King Gristle said.

The king slumped over in defeat. Prince Gristle looked off into the distance, feeling sad and lost. Bridget watched as he passed by again, feeling sorry for the young prince. Then she went back to scrubbing the cold stone floor.

Meanwhile, the Trolls had run all night, so the next morning found them in a forest far from Bergen Town. They stopped in the middle of a beautiful clearing. The sun shone on the green grass, a clear brook babbled nearby, and birds sang in the trees.

King Peppy climbed onto a large mushroom and addressed his fellow Trolls in a loud, resonant voice.

"Here! Right here! *This* is where we will rebuild

our civilization. This spot has everything we need. Fresh air! Clean water! And *sweet* acoustics!"

The word "acoustics" echoed through the forest: "Acoustics! Acoustics! Acoustics! Acoustics! Acoustics...."

The Trolls cheered! They *loved* this spot! It was perfect for their new home. Princess Poppy took out a little cowbell and started beating a bouncy rhythm on it. The Trolls went right to work building their new forest home, far away from the dangers of the mean, miserable, hungry Bergens.

Twenty years later, Princess Poppy had grown into a young adult Troll—now a full five inches tall! She loved reading to the Troll children from her beautiful, glittering scrapbook, telling them the story of the Trolls' escape from the Bergens. "From that day forward," she concluded, "no Troll ever had to worry about being eaten, ever again. King Peppy had made us safe."

The Troll children sitting at Poppy's feet smiled, looking at each other and nodding. Here in their forest home, they were safe from the Bergens!

Poppy looked up from her scrapbook. "And so

we are free to live in perfect . . . *harmony*!" She sang the last word in her lovely, clear voice.

One of the Troll children joined in, singing on a higher note that blended with Poppy's: *"Harmony!"* A second Troll child completed the chord, adding an even higher note: *"Harmony!"*

Another child raised her hand, and Poppy said, "Yes?"

"Is that why we hug every hour?" she asked.

"Yup!" Poppy said, nodding.

"I wish it was every *half* hour . . . ," a Troll child said, and several others nodded. That was a good idea! Hugs every half hour!

"So do I," Poppy agreed. "But that wouldn't leave much time for singing and dancing, now, would it?"

"Poppy's right!" the children said. "We *love* singing and dancing!"

"That's good," Poppy said, smiling, "because there's going to be lots and lots of singing and dancing at the party tonight. It's going to be the best party EVER!"

Old King Peppy joined the group. "I hope it's a *surprise* party!" he said with a grin.

The Troll kids were delighted to see their leader.

"King Peppy!" they cried. They all ran and jumped on the happy old Troll, holding on to his long pink mustache and his cloud of pink hair.

"Ha, ha!" King Peppy laughed. But his old bones couldn't handle the weight of so many Trolls anymore—even little ones. "All right, now," he said. "Get 'em off me, Poppy!"

Princess Poppy lovingly helped her dad up. One of the kids handed King Peppy the beautiful scrapbook. "Look what Princess Poppy made for you!" he said.

"Oh!" the king said, amazed. He flipped through the pages, admiring the pictures Poppy had made of the Trolls' escape from the Bergens. "Look at us!" he said. "Me and my little girl."

Then King Peppy looked up from the scrapbook and said, "Poppy, you know I'm not going to be around forever. Pretty soon you're going to be in charge."

His daughter looked doubtful. Was she ready to handle all that responsibility? Then she smiled and said, "Don't be silly! You're going to be around a long, long time. And anyway, today is all about you. You're my hero, Dad, and I want the whole world to know it."

King Peppy looked touched. Poppy turned to the kids. "That's why we're going to have *so much fun* tonight, right?"

"YAY!" they cheered. "SO MUCH FUN!"

"And I want *everybody* to be at the party!" Poppy announced.

"Everybody?" asked one of the young Trolls.

"Everybody!" Poppy answered as she pulled out her old cowbell and started to play a funky beat. Bubbling over with glee, the children danced.

CHAPTER 5

All the Trolls in the village danced and sang as they got ready for the big party.

Poppy paraded through Troll Village, handing out invitations to the celebration. She strutted and grooved with every step through the village.

A fuzzy pink-striped, giraffe-like Troll named Cooper kicked his blue legs and rapped. *"Awww, it ain't hard to be happy when you're doing it right! Put a smile on blast—that's the Troll life!"*

Poppy continued through the village, passing out more invitations. To a little yellow Troll named Smidge, Poppy rapped, *"Come on, Smidge! I know you can do it!"*

"Your confidence gives me STRENGTH!" Smidge

shouted happily as she used her long turquoise hair to give Poppy a boost, raising her way up above the crowd of Trolls. Poppy tossed invitations to everyone from high atop Smidge's hair.

During the excitement, a large blue Troll named Biggie took pictures of his pet worm, Mr. Dinkles. "Okay, Mr. Dinkles," Biggie coaxed, aiming his camera. "Say 'Leaves!'"

"*Mew!*" Mr. Dinkles mewed.

CLICK! Biggie took the picture. When he looked at it, he discovered that Poppy had slipped into the shot and given Mr. Dinkles a hug! Photobomb!

Pleased with the picture, Biggie slapped it into a frame and hung it on a wall beside hundreds of other pictures of Mr. Dinkles. "Hmm," he said, studying the new photo and stroking his chin. "Something's missing."

Dressed in nothing but glitter, Guy Diamond overheard Biggie. He stepped forward and farted a cloud of glitter onto the photo, making it sparkle! Biggie clapped his hands.

"That's it!" all the Trolls cried. They danced through the village, hanging decorations and adding glitter everywhere while they sang.

As they wound through the town, the Trolls joined hands with more of their friends: Satin and Chenille (two fashion-loving twins joined at the hairdo), Fuzzbert (all green hair and toes), and DJ Suki (sporting headphones). They sang about feeling the beat and about being united and about being all right!

They ended their song with a big finish, forming a giant Troll pyramid.

"YEAH!" Poppy shouted happily, breathing hard from all the dancing.

CLAP. CLAP. CLAP.

Someone was applauding their exhausting fun slowly and sarcastically.

CHAPTER 6

"**U**nbelievable, guys," the dull, sarcastic voice said. "Really great."

The voice belonged to Branch, a drab, serious gray Troll who had not taken part in the dancing and singing. In fact, he had never taken part in any singing, dancing, hugging, or fun for as far back as anyone could remember. "Good job," he continued. "I could hear you from a mile away."

"Oh, hey, Branch!" Poppy greeted him cheerfully. She jumped off the top of the Troll pyramid and landed gracefully in front of him. She knew Branch was different from the other Trolls, but she thought maybe if she tried hard enough, she could change that.

Still breathing hard, the other Trolls fell out of their pyramid formation. "*Oof!*"

"And if *I* could hear you," Branch went on, his

voice dropping to a cautious whisper, "so could the *Bergens*."

The Trolls rolled their eyes. They'd heard plenty of warnings like this from Branch before.

"OH, BOY," Guy Diamond sighed. His voice had a techno-reverby shimmer.

"Here we go again," Cooper said.

Biggie shook his head. "Oh, Branch."

"You always ruin everything . . . ," Satin chimed in.

". . . warning us about the nasty Bergens," Chenille finished.

Branch looked a little taken aback. "No, I don't," he insisted.

But they were right.

Like the time during a birthday party when Branch had run in screaming, "THE BERGENS ARE COMING! *AHHH!*" and pushed the birthday cake over. *SMOOSH!*

Or the time during a wedding party when he'd run in screaming, "THE BERGENS ARE COMING! *AHHH!*" and pushed the wedding cake over. *SPLAT!*

Or the time during a funeral when he'd run in screaming, "THE BERGENS ARE COMING! *AHHH!*" and pushed the casket over. *CLUNK!*

"Come on!" Poppy told Branch. "We haven't seen

a Bergen in twenty years. They're not gonna find us!"

"You know how to keep them from finding us?" he asked. "No more singing, no more dancing, and NO MORE PARTIES!" Branch insisted, angrily waving Poppy's homemade invitation in her face.

Cooper looked surprised. The giraffe-like Troll turned to Poppy. "You invited Branch to the party?"

"Of course I did," Poppy said. "'No Troll left behind,' remember?"

Branch looked disgusted. "Your dad wasn't talking about *parties* when he said that," he pointed out. "He was trying to keep us all *safe*."

But Poppy wasn't backing down. "And now that we *are* safe, I believe every Troll should be happy. Even you!"

"What are you going to do?" Branch asked. "*Force* me to be happy?"

Poppy shook her head. "No, but if you want the world to be a happy place, you start by being a happy person. Then that inspires someone else to be happy, and *they* inspire someone else, and then happiness spreads and spreads—"

"Like a disease?" Branch interrupted.

Poppy refused to let Branch's negative attitude bring her down. "Precisely! Happiness. You should try it!" Getting an idea, she grabbed the party invitation from Branch and opened it. When she took it out of its envelope, the invitation expanded like a pop-up book, showing a big celebration. Faint music and voices emanated from the tiny speaker in the card. Then a small paper Branch figure popped up. Poppy made cheerful a face at Branch that said *Isn't this great? How could you possibly say no to an invitation like this?* Finally, a little poof of glitter shot out of the card, landing anticlimactically on the ground in front of Branch.

Branch shook glitter off his feet. "I'm not going to the party," he said matter-of-factly.

All the Trolls looked shocked. How could anyone *not* go to a party?

"But it's gonna be the biggest . . . ," Satin and Chenille said together.

". . . the loudest . . . ," DJ Suki added.

". . . the craziest party ever!" Cooper shouted. They all cheered.

Branch shook his head in disbelief. "Big? Loud? Crazy? You're just going to lead the Bergens right to us! I wouldn't be caught dead at your party. But you will be—caught *and* dead!"

Poppy looked a little worried. Could Branch

possibly be right? She certainly didn't want to put the Trolls in any danger.

"Whoa, whoa . . . ," said a smooth voice. "Easy, guys, easy."

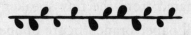

A calm, spiritual Troll seated in a full lotus position came floating in. His name was Creek. They all knew Creek was an amazing Troll who loved meditation and yoga and channeling good vibes, but was he actually *levitating*? Unbelievable!

No. Wait. He was actually sitting on a flying bug. He hopped off, pressed his hands together, and bowed to the bug. "Thank you for providing safe passage, brother," Creek said. The bug gave a modest little *buzz* and flew away.

Branch rolled his eyes. Creek wanted everyone to think he was totally centered and at one with himself and the universe. But Branch wasn't buying it. Not one bit.

Creek stepped over to Branch and gently placed a hand on his shoulder. "Okay, first of all, mate, thanks for sharing your unique perspective on things. Again. But just for now, why don't you try on some positivity, eh? A little positivity might go great with that vest."

The other Trolls nodded in agreement, and Creek looked smug. But Poppy knew Branch wasn't going to be convinced that easily.

"Look, Branch," she said, "I understand your concerns. I do. And I appreciate how vigilant you've always been. But we haven't seen a Bergen in twenty years. They're not going to find us."

Branch kicked a pebble away. "No, they're not going to find *me*, because I'll be living it up in my highly camouflaged, heavily fortified, Bergen-proof survival bunker."

"Sounds cozy," Creek said with smug sincerity.

Poppy started to answer Branch, but the flower bud strapped to her wrist opened, glowed, and chimed *DING!* "Hug Time!" she announced.

"It *is* Hug Time," Creek said, nodding.

"Hug Time!" squealed all the Trolls except Branch. They threw their arms around each other for a big group hug, squeezing Branch in the center of the clump.

"Ah, this hug feels good," Biggie sighed.

"Our hearts are synchronizing," Creek explained.

"I COULD SQUEEZE YOU GUYS FOREVER," Guy Diamond said.

"No!" Branch protested. He managed to wriggle

his way out of the bunch. Then he addressed Poppy. "Singing, dancing, hugging . . . *these* are your leadership skills? When we face a crisis, and the survival of every Troll is in your hands, I sure hope the answer is throwing a great party . . . because that's all you know how to do!" He shook his head. "I can't believe you're going to be queen one day."

Poppy looked hurt. Somehow Branch had known the exact thing to say that would hurt her the most—the very thing she'd been worrying about privately.

Branch stormed off. Cooper turned to Poppy. "Don't let Mr. McHater ruin the party."

Creek put a hand on Poppy's shoulder. "Hey," he said softly. "Branch *wants* to be miserable. It's what makes him happy."

"I guess . . . ," Poppy said uncertainly. *But how can you be happy if you're miserable?* she thought.

"You guessed right," Creek said. He playfully touched her nose. "Boop!" he said.

Poppy still wasn't sure what to do about Branch. But for now, there was a very big party to tend to.

CHAPTER 7

That evening, all the Trolls gathered in the palace, the biggest pod in the village. Cooper proudly walked onto a mushroom stage with King Peppy riding on his back. Poppy followed them. King Peppy hopped off Cooper's back and waved to the crowd. Everyone cheered!

"KING PEPPY! KING PEPPY! KING PEPPY!"

While gathering sticks nearby, Branch could hear the loud cheering. He knew the big celebration had begun. A tiny, secret part of him thought it might be just a little bit fun to be a part of it. But then he snorted in disgust, turned his back on the festivities, and headed for his underground bunker with his bundle of sticks.

Standing on the stage in front of the crowd, Poppy

could see how much the Trolls loved her dad. Feeling inspired, she turned to DJ Suki and pointed skyward with her thumb. "Turn the music up!" Poppy called. "Turn it UP!"

With her headphones on, DJ Suki couldn't hear Poppy. But she knew the signal. She turned the music up—WAY up! The bass pounded. *THUMP! THUMP! TH-TH-TH-TH-THUMP!*

Smidge loaded more glitter into the cannons on the edge of the stage. "More glitter!" Poppy shouted. "YEAH!" She was a big believer that you can never really have too much glitter.

BOOM! The cannons fired glitter into the air! It landed everywhere! Everything sparkled! When Smidge and a few other Trolls turned on huge multicolored spotlights, the glitter sparkled even brighter!

But the big, loud, crazy party was just getting started. *KA-BOOOOOM!* A gigantic glitter explosion went off, sending a huge shower of glitter into the night sky.

This party is SO wonderful! Everything's going great. I knew Branch was overreacting . . . again, Poppy thought.

Not too far away, in another part of the forest, someone had parked a beat-up camper van. When the thumping bass beats from the party had reached the van, the owner opened the door and stuck her head out, listening intently.

It was Chef.

For twenty years she'd been searching for the Trolls, hoping to regain her powerful position among the Bergens. And now she was hearing music that sounded exactly like the kind the Trolls loved!

Chef quickly climbed onto the top of her camper, passing the map where she'd X'd out the sections she'd already searched. She set up her telescope and started scanning the area, sweeping the scope in one direction and then the other, searching for a sign of Troll activity.

As she peered through the telescope, she heard the thump of a firework being shot into the air. *FWOOMP.* It burst into the night sky!

"A Troll!" growled Chef, delighted. After all these years, had she finally found those elusive, delicious Trolls?

Back in Troll Village, Poppy stepped to the front of the stage and held up her hands, signaling for everyone to listen.

"It's Poppy! She's my friend! I know her!" Biggie said. The other Trolls shushed him. Looking a little sheepish, he bit into a cupcake.

When the crowd had finally quieted down, Poppy took her father's hand and began to speak.

"I'd like to take a second to celebrate my father." She felt a thrill as the sky lit up with fireworks. Poppy knew that happiness really came from within, and the light from the fireworks was a reflection of that happiness. "Our king, who twenty years ago this night saved us all from those dreaded—"

BOOM. BOOM. BOOM. Poppy's speech was interrupted by an ominous stomping sound in the forest. And it was getting closer.

The Trolls looked at each other, worried. What could make a sound like that? It couldn't possibly be—

They looked up. The party lights hanging in the trees above them swayed as big footsteps shook the ground. A dark shadow loomed over them.

"BERGENS!" cried King Peppy.

CHAPTER
8

With terrible glee, Chef stomped into the clearing. "After all this time," she hissed, savoring every word. "Here you are! The Trolls! MY Trolls!"

Terrified, Cooper pooped out three tiny pink cupcakes. Poppy picked one up and nervously offered it to Chef. "Uhh," she said. "Cupcake?"

Chef snarled and unzipped the leather pouch she was wearing around her waist. *ZZZIP!*

"RUN!" Poppy shouted.

Screaming, the Trolls scattered in every direction. Poppy took her father by the hand and helped him get off the stage.

Biggie started to run, but realized he didn't know where his beloved worm was. "Mr. Dinkles!" he cried. "Has anybody seen Mr. Dinkles?"

As Biggie stood there, desperately looking around

for his pet, Poppy saw Chef rapidly approaching. "BIGGIE!" she yelled. He turned, and Poppy saw that Mr. Dinkles had somehow latched himself on to Biggie's back. Chef's big hand came down and scooped them both up in one quick motion.

Poppy ran through the crowd. "Blend in!" she instructed all the Trolls. "Blend in! Blend in!"

The Trolls used their hair and camouflaged their colors to blend in with their surroundings, but some of them weren't quick enough. Chef snatched up as many of them as she could grab, wearing a horrible, toothy grin.

Poppy watched helplessly as the cruel Bergen seized her friends. "Run, Smidge!" she cried.

"AHHHHH!" Smidge screamed.

Chef's hand closed around Smidge, but the little Troll managed to squeeze free between the Bergen's fingers. WHAP! Chef slapped her hand down on Smidge, stunning her like a bug. She scraped the Troll off the ground and dropped her into her leather pouch.

Panicking, Satin and Chenille tried to flee in opposite directions, but their shared hair made it impossible. Chef reached down, hooked her gnarled finger under the arch of the twins' hair, and lifted them up. *"AHHHHH!"* they screamed. Chef dropped them into her leather pouch with the other captured Trolls.

Poppy led the young Trolls she'd been reading to earlier toward a hiding spot in the bushes.

"Poppy, help!" cried a Troll named Harper.

"Hurry!" Poppy urged. "Quick—go, go, go!"

Cooper tried to hide, but his long neck betrayed him—his head stuck out of the bushes and Chef snatched him up. *"AHHHHH!"* Cooper screamed as Chef tossed him into her pouch.

"Cooper!" Poppy cried.

"Everyone!" Creek said. "Minimize your auras!"

Unfortunately, none of the Trolls knew how to do this. In fact, they weren't sure what their auras were. And even worse, Creek had caught Chef's attention. The hideous Bergen reached down to grab him. Her knobby hand clamped around the poor Troll and started to lift him away. Poppy rushed over to help.

"Creek!" she shouted.

"Poppy!" Creek called in a scared voice, stretching toward her.

Poppy shot her hair out, wrapping it around Creek's wrists. She tried with all her might to pull him out of Chef's tight grasp. "Hold on!" she gasped, straining to yank him free.

"Poppy!" Creek pleaded. "Help me! I'm feeling very . . . uncentered!"

But even with her amazing hair, the little Troll's strength was no match for the big Bergen's. Poppy's hair lost its grip. She watched, horrified, as Chef carried Creek away.

"NO!" he screamed. *"AHHHH!"*

Chef stuffed him into her pouch, keeping her eyes on the ground, searching for more Trolls to snatch. "Hmmm," she said, satisfied. She'd spotted one more—King Peppy. He was right by Chef's foot, whacking her toe with his cane.

"Bad Bergen!" he said sternly. "Bad, bad Bergen!"

Poppy saw that her father was about to be taken by the Bergen. "DAD!" she cried. She ran and grabbed him, and pulled him underneath the palace's mushroom stage. She had just enough time to blend in, using her hair as camouflage, hiding them both.

Chef turned toward the spot where she'd heard Poppy call to her dad. But no one was there. She squatted down and peered under the stage, but thanks to Poppy's camouflage, Chef could no longer see them. *"Hmmph,"* she said, straightening up.

The Bergen scanned the entire village, knocking over structures and destroying pods, but she couldn't find any more Trolls. She smiled an awful smile and announced, "Thanks for throwing the biggest, the loudest . . ."

". . . the CRAZIEST party ever!" Cooper said, sticking his head out of Chef's leather pouch. Chef scowled. *ZZZZIP!* She zipped the pouch closed as the Trolls inside wailed in protest. Ignoring their pleas, Chef stomped off into the woods. *BOOM. BOOM. BOOM. BOOM.* The ground shook. Leaves and branches fell from the trees. Birds flew off into the sky, squawking.

Then all was quiet.

Poppy's colors—pink and magenta—slowly returned to normal as she came out of her camouflage. So did King Peppy's. They rushed out from under the mushroom stage and ran to the center of the destroyed village. Other Trolls slowly emerged from hiding.

"Is it coming back?" one Troll asked nervously.

"What are we gonna do now?" Harper wailed.

"Everyone, *hurry*!" King Peppy said. "We have to leave before the Bergens come back. We must find a new home!" He started picking up young Trolls and hiding them in his hair.

But Poppy was still thinking about the Trolls Chef had carried off in her pouch. "Dad," she said urgently, "what about 'No Troll left behind'?"

King Peppy looked sad. "I'm sorry, Poppy. That was a long time ago, and I'm not the king I once was."

The remaining Trolls looked at each other in shock, thinking, *What are we going to do? Who's going to take care of us?*

"Which is why we have to run," King Peppy continued. "Let's go, everyone!" Waving his arms, he urged all the Trolls to get moving.

Poppy realized she had only one option.

"Then I'll go," she said. "I'll go and save my friends."

The others were speechless. An inexperienced princess on a dangerous rescue mission?

King Peppy stopped in his tracks. "Poppy," he said in a pained voice, "you can't go out there all alone."

Poppy started to protest, but an idea struck her. A wry smiled crossed her face, and she suddenly felt more confident. In fact, she felt downright brave. She knew she could do it.

"Oh, I won't be alone," she assured her father.

CHAPTER
9

Deep in his survival bunker, Branch sat alone at a table lit by a single dim lamp. He was surrounded by supplies—all the things he'd need to live by himself in the underground stronghold for a long, long time.

He was looking at his invitation to the party. He opened it, and a miniature version of himself popped out, holding a sign that read YOU'RE INVITED! An upbeat tune played from the handmade card.

The table was cluttered with other elaborate invitations sent by Poppy—invitations to birthday parties, weddings, and even funerals. Every one of them had a little Branch head sticking out of it. Branch had secretly kept every single one.

BANG! BANG! BANG!

Someone was knocking on his front door, up at

ground level! Embarrassed to be caught looking at Poppy's invitations, the gray Troll quickly tried to stuff them away, but they all started to play loud songs. *"Branch, you're invited!" "Come to my party, Branch!" "Branch, Branch, Branch!"*

"No, no, no!" Branch said. "Shhh! Shhh!"

Up by the entrance to Branch's bunker, Poppy was pounding on the door, calling, "Branch! Branch! Are you in there?" The entrance was just a big gray rock with a periscope on top so Branch could see who was at his door.

A welcome mat lay in front of the door. Unlike most welcome mats, this one said GO AWAY!

A metal latch in the mat slid open, and a pair of dark eyes peered out to see who was knocking. Poppy recognized those eyes.

"I'm not going to your party!" Branch barked.

"The party's over," Poppy said. "We just got attacked by a Bergen!"

"I knew it!" Branch said.

Poppy heard lots of locks being unlocked. A trapdoor opened, and Branch pulled Poppy inside. *WHUMP!* The trapdoor was closed tight.

In the gloomy entry to the bunker, Branch quickly

relocked all the locks and reset all his traps. He and Poppy sat there quietly in the dark, surrounded by traps.

"Branch, I—" Poppy started to say.

But Branch immediately shushed her. "Shhh!"

"I have to tell you—" she said.

"Shhhh!"

"I was just gonna—"

"Shhhhhhh!"

Poppy patiently raised her hand, as though she were waiting for a teacher to call on her.

Branch looked annoyed. "What?" he snapped. "What could be so important that it's worth leading the Bergen right to us?"

"The Bergen's gone," Poppy said.

"You don't know that! It could still be out there. Watching. Waiting." He lowered his voice to a barely audible whisper. "Listening."

"No, it *left*," Poppy insisted. Her voice rose. "And it took Cooper and Smidge and Fuzzbert and Satin and Chenille and Biggie and Guy Diamond . . ."

Branch looked very concerned.

". . . and Creek!"

Branch rolled his eyes. "Eh," he said, shrugging.

Poppy ignored Branch's reaction to the news of Creek's capture. "Which is why I have to ask you— will you go to Bergen Town with me and help me save everyone?"

Branch was so startled by the question that he jumped to his feet, accidentally tripping one of the traps. *SNAP!* That set off a chain reaction of closing traps. *SNAP! SNAP SNAP SNAP SNAP SNAP!*

"What?" Branch exclaimed, pulling one off his foot. "No."

Now it was Poppy's turn to look startled. "Branch, you can't say no! They're your friends!"

Branch held up a finger and shook his head. "Uh, uh, uh! They're *your* friends! I'm staying right here in my bunker, where it's safe." He turned his back on her and stubbornly folded his arms across his chest, careful not to step on another trap.

Poppy raised her arms in disbelief. "Oh, that's great. You're the one guy who knows more about Bergens than anyone, but when we finally need you, you just want to hide here forever?"

"Forever?" Branch repeated. He snorted. "No."

He pulled a lever. The platform he and Poppy were standing on began to descend. It sank lower and lower, passing shelves holding jars of liquid, food, and other supplies.

"Oh!" Poppy said, surprised. She'd never been in Branch's bunker before, so she hadn't realized there was more to it than the small, dark room they'd been standing in.

"Yeah," Branch said, speaking up so Poppy could hear him over the sound of the machinery that lowered the platform. "I really only have enough supplies down here to last me ten years. Eleven if I'm willing to store and drink my own sweat. *Which I am.*"

Poppy shuddered at the thought of drinking sweat. *Gross.* "Ugh," she groaned.

"You all said I was crazy, huh?" Branch continued. "Well, who's crazy now?"

THUMP. The platform landed at the bottom of the bunker. The lighting down there was a little brighter, so Poppy was able to see that the walls were covered in crazy writing, scribbling, and drawings, mostly of monstrous Bergens baring their fangs. Red strings were thumbtacked to the drawings, connecting them in ways that Poppy couldn't begin to understand. And there were shelves and shelves of supplies and more supplies.

"Me! Crazy-PREPARED!" Branch said proudly.

But Poppy wasn't impressed by Branch's preparations for a Bergen attack. In fact, he seemed a little nuts. "Branch," she pleaded, "you have to come with me. All the Trolls are looking to me to save them."

"No, they're not," Branch said.

"Okay, fine, they're not. But I'm all they've got."

"Why don't you try scrapbooking them to freedom?" Branch suggested sarcastically.

Poppy felt stung. "Solid burn, Branch."

She thought maybe he just wanted to tease her a bit before he'd give in and come with her. But he just stood there, looking like he was going nowhere for the next ten years. Eleven if he drank his own sweat.

"Well, thanks anyway," Poppy sighed.

"Hey, anytime, Poppy," Branch said. "See you in ten years. Or eleven. If you somehow survive, which seems unlikely."

Poppy sadly pulled the lever on the elevator platform and rose back up the angled tunnel.

Branch watched her go. He was left alone in the dim chamber. This gloomy underground bunker would be his only home for years. Though he didn't want Poppy to know it, he secretly dreaded the loneliness.

Light spilled into the room. Poppy was coming back!

"Oh, hey, Branch," she said casually. "Just wondering if I could borrow something."

"What?" he asked, rolling his eyes.

"Your bunker!"

"What?"

"Okay, everybody!" Poppy called up the tunnel. "Come on in!"

Before Branch could do a thing about it, all the Trolls who hadn't been captured by Chef came tumbling down the sloping tunnel into the bunker! *"WHEEEE!"* some of them squealed as they slid down the tube. When they reached the room at the bottom, they immediately began ransacking the shelves full of food and beverages.

"No!" Branch protested. "No! Whoa, whoa, whoa! Wait! Poppy, what are you doing?"

"You said you have enough provisions to last ten years, right?"

"Yes, to last *me* ten years! ME! It'll last THEM two weeks!"

Poppy smiled. "Then I guess I'd better hurry." She turned and started to head for the elevator.

"Wait, wait, wait!" Branch cried. "You're really going to Bergen Town on your own?"

"My father didn't leave any Trolls behind, and neither will I," Poppy vowed.

"But you won't last a day out there!"

"And *you* won't last a day in here," she answered, smiling. "Solid burn returned."

Branch had no answer for that. He watched helplessly as Poppy made her way through the crowd to her father.

"Goodbye, Dad," she said, trying to sound brave.

King Peppy grabbed his daughter and pulled her in for a big hug. "Good luck, Poppy," he said.

She smiled when they finished hugging. But as she walked toward the elevator platform, she also looked a little worried.

Poppy stepped onto the platform and turned to take one last look at all the Trolls in Branch's bunker. "Bye, everybody!" she said brightly, waving. "See you soon!"

"Bye, Princess Poppy!" they all cried, waving back.

Poppy pulled the lever and the platform started to rise up the slanted tunnel. She looked at the Hug Time watch on her wrist and began to count down the seconds, "And three . . . two . . . one . . ."

DING! Everyone's Hug Time watches bloomed and chimed, emitting a soft glow of colorful light.

"Ooh!" King Peppy said happily. "Hug Time!"

Branch looked around frantically, knowing what was coming—desperate to escape. Poppy smiled down at him and waved as she rose out of sight.

All the Trolls started slowly moving toward Branch with their arms outstretched like zombies. "Hug Time, Hug Time, Hug Time . . . ," they chanted as they closed in on the gray Troll.

"No . . . no . . . NO!" Branch yelled.

Outside, Poppy whipped out the scrapbooking materials she always carried with her and quickly used felt and glitter to illustrate the beginning of her journey. As her hands flew, she narrated the story aloud to herself.

"With her friends safely hidden, Princess Poppy set off to rescue her other friends, confident she'd make it to Bergen Town on her own." That didn't sound quite right to her. "Convinced *she'd make it to Bergen Town.*" No, that wasn't it. "Totally sure *she'd make it to Bergen Town.*" Much better!

Poppy closed her scrapbook, took a deep breath, and started to follow Chef's huge footprints through the forest.

Soon she was in unfamiliar territory. The canopy of leaves overhead was thicker than the forest she was used to, so less sunlight broke through and the woods were darker. The plants on the ground looked odd. A strange bird gave a frightening cry.

To calm herself, Poppy sang a song about being brave. Facing danger. Rescuing her friends. *"I mean, how hard can that be?"*

She was standing on a huge flower above a field of gigantic, colorful blooms. *SNAP!* The flower broke, and Poppy fell!

But before she crashed to the ground, she extended her hair down, forming it into a stairway. She gracefully landed on the steps and walked down to the ground, still singing her song.

A colorful butterfly fluttered just above her head, so Poppy incorporated a few lines about it into her song. But then a bizarre-looking creature shot out its tongue and gobbled up the butterfly.

Immediately, that creature was eaten by a brutish beast as it flew by—

That was in turn zapped with fire by a strange-looking plant. All in a matter of seconds!

Still, Poppy kept singing her optimistic song, no matter what scary things were going on around her. She bounced along on orange puffballs, blown into the sky by their puffs. She landed on a long snake, patterned like a scarf or a pair of socks, and slid along its long back, running away from it. She fell through the sky and tried to escape from a hungry bird. The bird swallowed her whole and then laid an egg in its nest. Poppy hatched out of the egg but had to fight off the bird's other two hatchlings.

She kept singing: *"Get back up again!"*

Poppy rode a leaf, suffering through the heat of a sandy desert and the cold of ice and snow. Underwater, she passed through an enormous fish. She bounced across bouncing eyeballs. She landed in a plant with lots of eyes sticking up on stalks and sharp teeth lining its big mouth. She pried its jaws open and escaped, only to be eaten by an even bigger plant.

Still, she kept singing. *"Get back up again!"*

Poppy fell through a long, dark shaft, but before she hit the bottom, she used her hair to grab two walls and break her fall. Her hair acted like springs, slingshotting her out of the tunnel. *SPROING!*

But she kept singing. *"Get back up again!"*

Poppy ate what looked like a blueberry. Blue spots appeared on her face and her body. She swelled up until she was a big blue ball that rolled away.

Singing . . .

Poppy fell through a series of sticky white spiderwebs, becoming more wrapped up the more she struggled—until she looked like a mummy. She hit the ground completely cocooned, and though she was still singing, she was exhausted.

She sighed and passed out.

In the dark shadows, multiple black eyes glimmered.

When the small figure wrapped in webbing ceased to move, they crept forward. Seeing their chance, three giant hairy spiders emerged from the darkness and closed in on Poppy. She looked like a tasty morsel, and the hungry creatures gnashed their teeth in anticipation of a good meal as they moved closer and closer and closer to the helpless Troll. . . .

CHAPTER
10

BONK! One of the spiders got walloped on the head with a heavy iron frying pan! All the spiders turned and saw . . .

. . . Branch!

"RRROOOAAR!" The spiders advanced on Branch with their front legs raised, ready to attack.

Branch whirled his long hair around and whipped it at them. *SNAP! SNAP!* By using his hair as a whip, he was able to drive the monstrous spiders away. "Back! Get back! *Hyah! Hyah!* Get back!" Then . . .

GULP! They were swallowed up by a big creature that was just waiting for three delicious spiders to come along.

Branch enjoyed his victory for a moment. But then he saw Poppy on the ground, bound by the spiders' white silken cords. "Oh, no!" he gasped. "Poppy?"

Branch rushed to Poppy's side and used a bug like a pair of scissors—its sharp teeth and strong jaws cut her free from the spiderwebs. He checked for her vital signs. "Hang on!" he said. Then he used two bugs like electric paddles to zap her awake. *ZAP!*

Poppy immediately sat up, singing, *"Get back up again!"* Then she noticed Branch kneeling next to her, looking concerned. "Branch, my man! You are right on time!"

Branch couldn't believe what he was hearing.

"Oh, don't even!" he said. "Like you knew I was coming." He let the two zapping bugs go and they scurried away.

Picking strands of spiderweb out of her headband, Poppy stood up. "Obviously. I figured after the third Hug Time, getting eaten by a Bergen wouldn't seem so bad."

"What?" Branch said. *How could she possibly have known that I left right after the third Hug Time?*

"All right!" Poppy said confidently, starting to walk off. "Let's do this! The sooner we get to Bergen Town, the sooner we can rescue everybody and make it home safely."

Branch trotted after her. "Wait, wait, wait. *What's*

your plan?" he demanded.

"I just told you," Poppy said over her shoulder. "To rescue everyone and make it home safely."

"Okay, that's not a plan," Branch pointed out. "That's a wish list."

Poppy stopped and turned to face Branch, her fists on her hips. "Oh, I suppose *you* have a plan?"

Branch cleared his throat and paced, gesturing with his hands. "First we get to the edge of Bergen Town without being spotted. Then we get inside by sneaking through the old escape tunnels, which will then lead us to the Troll Tree, right before we get caught and suffer a miserable death at the hands of a horrible, bloodthirsty Bergen!"

He stopped pacing and looked around for Poppy. She was on the ground, cutting felt with scissors. "Hold on a second," he said. "Are you *scrapbooking* my plan?"

"Uh-huh," Poppy said, concentrating. "Yeah, almost, and . . . done!" She put the finishing touches on her scrapbook and beamed proudly at Branch. A little figure popped up out of the scrapbook and sang, *"We did it!"*

POOF! A burst of glitter shot out of the book,

covering Branch. "I changed your terrible ending, though," she said.

Branch stood for a moment in silence. Then: "There will be no more"—he paused to spit glitter out of his mouth—"scrapbooking!"

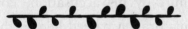

As they made their way through the dense forest, Branch couldn't help being annoyed by Poppy's relentless cheerfulness. "Do you have to sing?" he demanded at one point.

"I always sing when I'm in a good mood," she said. She resumed humming and singing to herself.

"Do you *have* to be in a good mood?" Branch asked.

"Why wouldn't I be?" Poppy countered. "By this time tomorrow, I'll be with all my friends!" She swung up onto a big fallen tree and started to make her way across it.

Adjusting his backpack, Branch followed her onto the tree. "Yeah," he said gloomily. "In a Bergen's stomach."

Poppy shook her head. "They're alive, Branch. I *know* it!"

"You don't know anything, Poppy," Branch insisted. "And I can't wait to see the look on your face when you realize the world isn't all cupcakes and rainbows. Because it isn't! Bad things happen, and there's nothing you can do about it."

A little hurt by his accusation, Poppy stopped for a moment. Branch passed her on the fallen tree. Then she ran to catch up with him. "I would rather be optimistic, happy, and, yes, *wrong* every once in a while than be like you. You don't sing, you don't dance . . . you're so gray all the time! What happened to y—"

Branch held up one hand. "Shhh!"

Poppy stopped in her tracks, her eyes wide. "What is it?" she whispered. "A Bergen?"

"Maybe," Branch whispered. He inched forward cautiously. When he was sure Poppy couldn't see his face, he smiled mischievously.

Poppy followed him quietly, then realized something. "There's no Bergen, is there? You just said that so I'd stop talking."

"Maybe," Branch whispered, and kept walking.

Poppy invites her Troll Village friends to a **crazy-awesome party**—but grumpy Branch worries they'll attract the Troll-eating Bergens!

Poppy visits Branch's bunker to ask him to help rescue her friends after a Bergen finds **Troll Village**.

Poppy takes the remaining Trolls to Branch's bunker for their safety. Horrified by Hug Time, Branch chooses to go with Poppy rather than stay.

Hugfest

Nothing can keep **Poppy** from saving her friends . . .

Poppy

. . . except some very scary spiders. But Branch arrives just in time! Now Poppy **KNOWS** they will succeed! Branch is less sure.

WE DID IT!!!

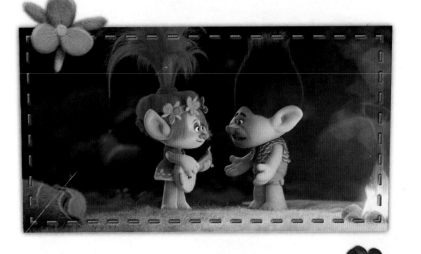

After a night in the forest, Poppy and Branch meet **Cloud Guy.** He helps Poppy and Branch find Bergen Town—all for the low price of one high five!

The Bergens are miserable without **Trollstice**, their one day of happiness. Chef and King Gristle hope to bring Trollstice back to Bergen Town by eating the Trolls!

About to be served by Chef, Poppy and the other Trolls give up hope and turn gray. But then Branch starts to sing. . . . Can he save the Trolls and return them to their **true colors**?

CHAPTER
11

That night, Poppy and Branch found a small clearing in the woods. They built a campfire and spread their sleeping bags out on the ground. Their fire made a small circle of light in the big, dark forest.

Before she went to sleep, Poppy took out a framed picture. As she expanded it, pulling out more and more frames, she revealed pictures of all the Trolls who'd been taken by Chef. She gently stroked the picture of Cooper, the giraffe-like Troll. "So special . . ."

Branch thought she'd go to sleep then, but instead she said good night to each of her friends in the expanding picture frame, one by one. "Good night, Cooper. Good night, Smidge. Good night, Fuzzbert. Good night, Satin. Good night, Chenille. Good night, Biggie. Good night, DJ. Good night, Guy Diamond.

Good night, Creek." She tapped Creek's nose in the photo. "Boop."

That was all Branch could take. "And *good night,* Poppy!" he growled, turning his back on her.

Poppy snuggled down into her sleeping bag. Branch remained alert, scanning the forest for danger.

DING! Poppy's Hug Time watch opened and softly chimed. She instinctively looked around for someone to hug, but Branch kept his back turned to her. "Don't. Even. Think about it," he said firmly.

Without a hug at bedtime, Poppy felt lost. She looked up at the twinkling stars and started to sing softly. *"Stars shining bright above you—"*

Branch turned around, exasperated. "Really? Seriously? More singing?"

"Yes, seriously!" Poppy answered. "Singing helps me relax. Maybe you ought to try it."

"I don't relax. This is the way I am, and I like it! I also like a little *silence*!"

The word "silence" gave Poppy an idea. She pulled out a mandolin, strummed a chord, and began to sing to Branch.

As Poppy sang, flowers, caterpillars, and strange woodland creatures all joined in, coming out of the darkness and into the campfire's flickering light. A cute, fuzzy little spider lowered itself onto Branch's shoulder and whispered into his ear. Branch scowled and without even looking at it, flicked the spider away. When the song was finished, the creatures faded back into the night.

Branch's expression softened and he extended his hand to Poppy, asking for the mandolin. "May I?"

Thinking he was finally going to play and sing, Poppy handed him the instrument. But he tossed it onto the fire! Then he got back into his sleeping bag before the look of surprise had even left Poppy's face.

As usual, Poppy made the best of things. She warmed her hands by the blazing fire. "So toasty!" she enthused.

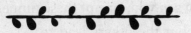

The next morning, Poppy and Branch reached the edge of the forest. They stood before a series of tunnels that led into a darkly forested mountainside. And somewhere beyond that was Bergen Town.

"So one of these tunnels leads to the Troll Tree," Poppy said. "There are so many of them. I wonder which one."

"I don't know," Branch said.

From out of nowhere, a deep, dramatic voice echoed around them: "Choose a hole wisely! For one will lead to Bergen Town. And the others to . . . *CERTAIN DEATH!*"

Branch and Poppy looked around, trying to see who had spoken. "Who said that?" Branch said loudly.

The deep voice spoke again: "It was"—there was a clearing of a throat, and the voice became higher and much less dramatic—"me!"

From behind a tree appeared Cloud Guy, a walking, talking cloud with big teeth, big blue eyes, skinny blue arms and legs, and striped gym socks on his feet. He gave them a friendly wave. "Hey, guys! How's it going? Welcome to the root tunnels. I just wanted to warn you, one of these tunnels leads to the Troll Tree, but the others lead to . . ." He switched back to his booming, dramatic voice: "CERTAIN *DEATH!*" He even made his own echo. "Death, death, death, death . . ."

Branch and Poppy exchanged a look. They'd never met a cloud before.

"Do you think you can tell us which tunnel is the right one?" Poppy asked in her friendliest voice.

"You bet!" Cloud Guy bubbled.

"Great!" Poppy said.

"No, that's okay," Branch said. "We're fine, thanks."

Poppy took Branch aside and spoke to him quietly. "Branch, he's trying to help us."

"I don't like the looks of him," Branch said suspiciously.

They snuck a glance back at Cloud Guy. He was picking his teeth. He waved again.

"He seems to know what he's talking about," Poppy argued.

"Okay, fine," Branch said, giving in. He turned back to Cloud Guy. "Which tunnel do we go in?"

Cloud Guy grinned. "First you have to give me a high five. Then I'll tell you."

"What?" Branch asked, taken aback. He hated high fives.

"Oh, oh! I *love* high fives!" Poppy said. "I'll do it!"

"Oh, I know *you'll* do it," Cloud Guy said. "But will he?"

Branch groaned.

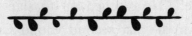

Cloud Guy stood there with his hand in the air, waiting for Branch to high-five him. "All right, Dumpy Diapers, up high!"

Branch shook his head. "Nope. I don't do high fives."

"Slap it, boss," Cloud Guy urged.

"Not gonna happen."

"Come on, just one little high five."

"Oh, no thanks. I'm good."

"Here. Just do this," Cloud Guy said, reaching up to slap his own hand. "But with *your* hand."

"Thank you for demonstrating," Branch said dryly. "Really cleared up exactly what I will *not* be doing."

Poppy pleaded with Branch. "It's a high five! The other tunnels lead to certain death! Get some perspective here!"

Smiling, Cloud Guy waited with his hand in the air.

Branch sighed. "ONE high five, and then you'll tell us which tunnel to take, right?"

"So easy," Cloud Guy whispered.

"*Grrr,*" Branch growled through gritted teeth. "Okay, fine!" He reached up to slap Cloud Guy's hand, but at the last second Cloud Guy yanked it away. Branch glared at him.

"*Whoop!* Too slow!" Cloud Guy said.

"Too slow?" Branch repeated in disbelief.

"Ha, ha!" Cloud Guy laughed, enjoying his own joke. Then he composed himself. "All right. I'm gonna let you slide with a fist bump."

Branch moved his fist toward Cloud Guy's fist, but Cloud Guy quickly went through a bunch of hand moves, doing anything and everything but bumping his fist against Branch's. "*Whoop,* shark attack! *Nom, nom, nom!* Jellyfish! *Hand* sandwich! Turkey! Snowman! Dolphin! Helicopter! Last supper! Monkey in a zoo!"

"What?" Branch said, utterly baffled by all the jokey moves.

Finally, Cloud Guy offered his fist as if he was finally done messing around. But when Branch tried to bump it, Cloud Guy grabbed Branch's fist and yanked it down like a car's stick shift. "Gearshift!" He moved Branch's arm, making engine sounds. *"BRRRRM! VRRRM! BRRRRRM! BRUUM!"*

When he was finished, he chuckled. So did Poppy.

"Okay, okay, okay," Cloud Guy said, still laughing. "Now I'm thinking we hug."

Branch said nothing. He scowled, picked up a stick, and broke it in half. *Snap!* He aimed the two pointy ends at Cloud Guy as if they were daggers.

Cloud Guy turned as gray as a thundercloud. Trembling with fear, he rained a puddle onto the ground.

Yelling, Branch chased the screaming cloud around the edge of the forest.

"Branch!" Poppy shouted, running after him. "No! Wait!"

"That's right! You better run, cloud!" Branch threatened. "I'm gonna tear your little cloud arms off your cloud body and high-five your *face* with them!"

"Wait! No! He's just a cloud! He can help us!" Poppy yelled.

But Branch kept chasing Cloud Guy, waving his pointy sticks. "Get back here!"

"He's just a cloud!" Poppy repeated. "Run, Cloud Guy, run!"

They followed Cloud Guy into one of the tunnels and chased him all the way up to the end. Then Cloud Guy stopped, turned around, and faced the two panting Trolls. "*Ta-da!* We're here!"

Poppy and Branch realized Cloud Guy was right.

They'd reached the top of the Troll Tree!

"Whew," Cloud Guy said. "You guys are a lot of fun. You know, I gotta go. Got some cloud stuff to take care of. Catch you on the way back? Unless"— he switched back to his booming, dramatic voice— "YOU *DIE*!"

Cloud Guy zoomed away, back through the tunnel. Branch and Poppy looked at the Troll Tree. It was bare and leafless. The cage around it had long since rusted away.

"Whoa," Poppy said.

"The Troll Tree," Branch said, hardly able to believe they were actually there.

Below them, in the town surrounding the old tree, the Bergens went about their miserable business, chanting about how miserable they were without Trolls and Trollstice. One Bergen chopped on some blooming flowers. Another swatted at biting flies. A Bergen child dragged a kite through the mud. A grown-up Bergen tore pages out of a book.

One Bergen even shoveled dirt onto his chest, burying himself before he was dead.

"Wow," Poppy said. "They're as miserable as you." Then she realized something. "Which means they haven't eaten a Troll yet! Come on! Let's go save our friends!"

"*Your* friends," Branch corrected her.

"*Our* friends," Poppy repeated. "Don't fight it."

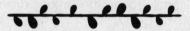

Inside the castle, King Gristle II—who had been Prince Gristle back when the Trolls escaped—slouched miserably on his throne beneath a big portrait of his father, King Gristle I. While Bridget the scullery maid scrubbed the floor, King Gristle II spoke to his pet alligator, Barnabus.

"Oh, Barnabus. You're my only friend in this whole miserable world."

Barnabus bit his hand.

"*Ow!*" the king yelped. "Dad was right. I'll never, ever, never, ever, *never* be happy." He collapsed over the arm of his throne. "*Never!*"

"Never say never," replied a figure emerging from the shadows.

CHAPTER 12

"AAAHH!" cried King Gristle, startled.

Guards held up their spears to stop the advancing figure, but Chef walked right past them, tossing her cloak onto their spears as she passed.

"Chad. Todd," she said, acknowledging their presence in a cold, formal voice.

When she spoke, King Gristle recognized her. "Chef? Where did you come from? My father banished you twenty years ago! Have you been standing behind that plant this whole time?"

Chef tried to put on her best humble face. "No, sire. I've been out in the wilderness, thinking of nothing but how I let you down. If only there were some way I could make you feel better."

The king dropped his chin into his hands. "Well,

fat chance! The only way I'll ever be happy is by eating a Troll, and that ain't gonna happen, thanks to you."

Chef gave a triumphant little smile. "Ah, but it just might," she said. "Thanks to me."

ZZZZIP! She unzipped her leather pouch, revealing the captured Trolls. A rainbow of light shone on the king's astonished face as he peered into the pouch. The Royal Guards dropped their weapons in shock. ZZZZIP! Chef closed the bag.

"You found the Trolls?" King Gristle exclaimed.

Chef just smiled and patted her leather pouch. Wild-eyed and salivating, King Gristle reached toward the pouch, but Chef slapped his hand away.

"So this means," King Gristle said, "I might actually get to be happy!"

"That's right," Chef confirmed. "Of course, everyone else in Bergen Town will still be miserable, but that's not your concern."

Disappointed by this news, the Royal Guards slumped. King Gristle noticed and felt bad for them. "I *am* their king," he said, "so maybe it kinda is my concern."

Chef pretended to be intrigued by what the king was saying. "What exactly are you proposing?

Bringing back Trollstice . . . for everyone?"

"Hmmm," the king said, thinking. "Yes, that's EXACTLY what I'm proposing!"

Chef acted impressed. "Great idea, sire! Absolutely brilliant! Aren't you smart?"

This is going perfectly, Chef thought. If the king brought back Trollstice, then she would get her job back. And the closer she was to the king, the more power *she* had.

"I guess I am!" King Gristle said, surprised. No one had ever suggested that to him before.

She put her arms on his shoulders, picked him up, and spun him around so that she ended up sitting in the throne, not him. "And I, your loyal Chef, will be right behind you!" Under her breath, she added, "Holding a knife."

"Whazzat?" King Gristle asked, still thinking about how smart he was.

"Holding a knife," Chef said, "a spoon, and a ladle. I'm your Bergen Chef, after all!"

"Yeah," King Gristle agreed. "You sure are."

Chef smiled. Everything was going exactly according to her plan.

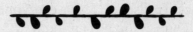

In one of the castle's hallways, two Royal Guards walked past each other on patrol. "Chad," said Todd.

"Todd," said Chad.

Poppy and Branch emerged from inside a sconce and snuck down the corridor. "So where do you think our friends are?" Poppy whispered.

"If I had to guess," Branch whispered, "I'd say . . . in a Bergen's stomach."

"Could you try to be positive? Just once? You might like it!"

Branch sarcastically spoke in a super-positive tone. "Okay, I'm sure they are not only *alive,* but about to be delivered to us on a *silver platter*!"

"Thank you!" Poppy said, not catching his sarcasm. "That wasn't so hard, was it?"

Her Hug Time watch chimed. *Ding!* Poppy smiled. "Branch!"

"Hug Time?" he said. "Really?"

"Shhh!" she said. "Listen!"

Branch listened. In the distance, he could hear the captured Trolls' Hug Time watches chiming!

But as he and Poppy started to move toward the

sound, Chef and Bridget walked into the hallway. Branch and Poppy hid while the Bergens passed. Chef's leather pouch glowed with the light of the Trolls' chiming Hug Time watches.

"Come on," Chef commanded, leading Bridget into the kitchen.

Clap! Clap! In the kitchen, Chef clapped her hands and torches ignited, lighting up the room. She grabbed a knife and pointed it at Bridget.

"You, scullery maid," she snarled. "What's your name?"

"Bridget."

"Congratulations, *Idget*—you work for me now." Chef gestured toward a huge pile of dirty dishes. "So you take those dishes downstairs and you start scrubbing!"

"Yes, Chef," Bridget said, picking up a towering pile of pots and pans. "Thank you, Chef." She left the kitchen, carefully balancing the greasy stack.

Chef joyfully waved her knife through the air. "I'm back!" she crowed. And with that, she unzipped her leather pouch and dumped the terrified Trolls into a cage.

CHAPTER
13

Inside the cage, the Trolls were freaking out.

"Whoa, whoa, everyone," Creek said in his most reassuring voice. "Just calm down. Get your Chakras aligned. . . ."

All the Trolls pulled out their combs and begin to meditate while combing their hair. "*Cooooomb,*" they chanted.

Chef leaned down and peered into the cage. "That's right, relax. A calm Troll is a tasty Troll. And you are a key ingredient in my recipe for success."

Shwik! Shwik! Shwik! Shwik! Chef sharpened her long knife on a steel rod.

"You see, he who controls the Trolls controls the kingdom," she gloated. "And I . . . I am that he!"

Cooper popped up. "You're a dude?"

"I *knew* it!" DJ Suki said.

Chef grabbed a lemon, cut a wedge, and squirted juice in Cooper's face. *"AHHH!"* the giraffe-like Troll yelled.

Chef felt triumphant as she began to flip through a cookbook called *Cookin' Trolls the Chef Way.* Soon she'd regain all her power and secretly be in charge of the Bergen kingdom—*no matter what that stupid King Gristle thinks.* She broke into hideous laughter. Thunder crashed! Lightning flashed! A crow cawed in the distance!

And in their cage, the Trolls huddled together, shuddering.

The castle's banquet hall hadn't been used in twenty years, so Bergens were scrubbing and polishing, trying to restore the long room to its former glory.

Poppy and Branch snuck down a chain hanging from the ceiling and hid in a chandelier, spying on the Bergens and trying to put together a rescue plan.

"That was such a great idea that I had!" King Gristle bragged as he entered the hall. "This is gonna be the best Trollstice *ever*." He paused to inspect the progress a couple of servants were making in their cleaning. "All right! Looks good. Real fancy!"

He turned and addressed everyone in the room. "Tomorrow is Trollstice, everyone! And it must be perfect." To himself he added, "It feels *great* to be ordering everyone around again."

Chef entered the banquet hall pushing a cart. The cart carried the Troll cage on a platter. "Branch, look!" Poppy whispered, pointing.

"They're alive?" Branch said. He couldn't believe it. He was sure they'd been eaten by Bergens.

"*And* on a silver platter, too!" Poppy said. "We were *both* right!"

Chef opened a wooden box and took out a bib. "Look, Your Highness," she exclaimed. "I found your old Troll bib!"

"Oh, wow!" King Gristle said. "I bet it still fits!"

But when he tried to fasten the bib around his neck, it was tight. *Really* tight. So tight, he could hardly breath. By pushing aside his neck fat, however, he managed to snap the bib's strap closed.

"*Ta-da!*" he said in a hoarse whisper.

"Very regal, sire," Chef said smugly.

RRRRIP! The bib tore apart, which knocked the king's crown off his head and sent it clattering to the ground.

From inside the cage, Cooper couldn't help laughing at the king. "HA, HA, HA, HA!"

"*Shhhh!*" warned the other Trolls.

The king stared at Cooper. "Oh, you think that's funny? Well, we'll see who's laughing when I bite your yummy head off! When I bite all y'all's yummy heads off!"

Then King Gristle noticed something disturbing. "Wait a minute," he said. "Chef, this isn't enough yummy heads to feed all of Bergen Town! How are we supposed to have Trollstice if there aren't enough Trolls?"

"There's *plenty* more where those came from, sire," Chef said, trying to reassure him.

"Are you sure?" he asked. "Because I promised everyone a Troll."

Seeing her plan unraveling, Chef decided this called for something dramatic.

"No, no, no, sire!" she said. "Everything will be fine! If I were truly worried, would I be willing to do *this*?" She reached into the cage and grabbed the first

Troll her claws touched—Creek.

"Creek!" Poppy squeaked, horrified.

Chef looked up toward the sound, but all she saw was the chandelier. She turned back to the king and shoved Creek into his hand.

"My first Troll," King Gristle said, amazed that the moment had finally come.

"Go on, eat, King Gristle," Chef urged. "Enjoy a taste of true happiness."

The king dangled the terrified little Troll above his open mouth. . . .

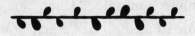

Then King Gristle hesitated. He turned to Chef. "Shouldn't we wait for Trollstice?"

All the Trolls breathed a huge sigh of relief. King Gristle tried to hand Creek back to Chef, but she pushed the Troll toward his face.

"Sire, *every* day is Trollstice when you have Trolls!" she insisted. She took Creek, stuck him in a taco shell, and handed him to the king.

The Trolls watched, horrified.

"Yeah, I guess," King Gristle said, slowly raising the taco to his mouth. He stopped. "But my dad said the first time should be special."

Poppy and Branch breathed another sigh of relief.

Remaining calm, Chef said, "Well, you *are* the king now." She drizzled some taco sauce on Creek.

"Yeah," King Gristle agreed. "I *am* the king!"

Chef shoved the Creek taco back toward Gristle's mouth. He was finally about to eat it, but he stopped again at the last second. "But I think I should share this moment with *all* the kingdom."

"EAT IT!" shouted Chef, losing what little patience she had to begin with. She crammed the Creek taco into King Gristle's open mouth. Creek yelped as the king snapped his mouth shut.

The Trolls gasped.

King Gristle cried out in ecstasy.

"Oh my gah!" Smidge said.

"No!" Poppy cried up in the chandelier.

"Yes," Chef said, smiling. Chef snapped her fingers, and the guards placed a sombrero on King Gristle's head and a maraca in each of his hands. Festive mariachi music began to play, and the guards twirled King Gristle toward the door with Creek in his mouth.

Chef smiled. Mission accomplished. "Idget," she

said, "you lock these Trolls in your room and guard them with your life." She hurled a spoon at Bridget, hitting her square in the head.

"Yes, Chef," Bridget replied meekly.

Chef escorted the king out of the banquet hall. *"Oooohhh!"* he cooed with his mouth full.

"Yes, yes, I know," Chef said.

King Gristle twirled down the hall blissfully.

Looking shell-shocked, Poppy turned to Branch. "We have to save him," she said.

"Save him from what?" Branch asked. "His stomach?"

"We didn't see him chew," Poppy said confidently. "We didn't see him swallow."

Branch shook his head. "Face it, Poppy. Sometimes people go into other people's mouths and they don't come out. If we go after Creek now, we're going to get eaten."

Looking stricken, Poppy watched the king walk joyfully down the hallway.

"I'm sorry," Branch said, "but it's too late for Creek."

Bridget was carrying the Troll cage out of the hall. As he watched the scullery maid dash off, Branch realized Poppy was no longer beside him.

"Poppy!" he called.

Poppy slid down a ladder and landed on Bridget's apron strings. Branch had no choice but to follow, and they both hitched a ride on Bridget's apron as she headed down to her room.

Bridget carried the cage into her dark little bedroom and set it on her nightstand. She took off her apron and hung it up.

Above her, Chef called, "Scullery maid!"

A trapdoor in the ceiling opened, and dirty dishes fell onto Bridget. *CRASH!*

"Wash these pots and pans for Trollstice!" Chef bellowed through the opening. "The king's inviting everyone—everyone except *you*."

Clunk. One last filthy pot landed on Bridget's head. She hurled herself onto her lumpy little bed and started to cry.

Then she began to sing. Poppy and Branch peeked out of a pocket in her apron. Bridget continued her bittersweet song as she pulled a stack of magazines out from under her bed. She flipped through them, looking for pictures of King Gristle. When she found one, she cut it out and stuck it on a part of her wall that was hidden behind a curtain. There were hundreds of them. Together they made one gigantic picture of the king.

When she'd gone through all the magazines, Bridget pulled out a pillow with the king's face on it. She kissed his lips gently, laid her head down, and fell asleep.

Poppy turned to Branch and whispered, "Bridget's in love with the king!"

CHAPTER
14

"**W**hat are you talking about?" Branch said. "Bergens don't have feelings!"

"Well, maybe you don't know everything about the Bergens," Poppy said, climbing out of the apron. "Now let's go!"

They quickly reached the Trolls on the other side of Bridget's room and yanked the cover off their cage. "Guys!" Poppy said.

"Poppy!" the Trolls cried, amazed and delighted to see their princess. They burst into song. *"Cel-e-brate good times, come on!"*

Caught up in the happy moment, Poppy joined them. *"It's a celebration!"*

"Shhh!" Branch shushed frantically.

The Trolls kept singing, but quieter, lowering their singing to a whisper. *"There's a party going on right here—"*

"No!" Branch whispered fiercely. "There is NOT a party going on right here!"

The Trolls stopped singing. Branch used Poppy's scrapbooking scissors to undo the latch on their cage. "The sooner we get you guys out of here—"

"The sooner we can save Creek!" Poppy announced.

"WHAT!" Branch said way too loudly, and then caught himself. But it was too late. Bridget sat up in bed. All the Trolls froze.

"Mmm, King Gristle," Bridget murmured. She fell back onto her pillow, sound asleep. The Trolls breathed a sigh of relief.

Branch spoke quietly to Poppy. "I know you're looking for the cupcakes and rainbows here, but let's face it—Creek's been eaten!"

"It was horrible," Cooper moaned.

"They put him in a taco!" Biggie said.

"SORRY, POPPY," Guy Diamond added. "CREEK'S GONE."

"Poppy," Branch said gently, "how could you possibly think he's still alive?"

With a determined look on her face, Poppy turned to Branch. "I don't *think* he's alive," she stated firmly. "I *hope* he is. And that's enough."

"How do you always look on the bright side?" Branch asked. "There is no bright side here. None!"

"There's *always* a bright side!" Poppy insisted.

Suddenly, the whole room brightened! Bridget had snapped on a light, and now her face was right down by the Trolls! To the tiny Trolls, she was a giant.

"Hey!" she said. "Where do you think you're going?"

The Trolls screamed and scattered throughout the room, looking desperately for places to hide.

"No!" Bridget yelled. "Get back in your cage! No! Chef's gonna be so mad!"

She cornered Branch next to a pile of dishes and raised a frying pan, ready to whack him.

"Bridget, *stop*!" Poppy said fiercely.

Bridget froze.

"You're in love with King Gristle," Poppy announced. She scampered across Bridget's bed and stopped in front of the curtain that hid the pictures of her crush.

"I don't know what you're talking about," Bridget

claimed, and she started to bring the frying pan down on Branch.

Poppy yanked back the curtain, revealing all the pictures of King Gristle.

"Uh, excuse me!" Bridget said. "That's not mine!"

Poppy pulled the curtain back a little farther, revealing a picture of Bridget looking up at the king with love in her eyes.

Bridget realized that her secret was out. "Oh, what does it matter?" she sighed. "It's not like he even knows I'm alive."

Poppy cautiously took a step closer to the sad scullery maid. "Bridget, I can help you! What if there's a way that we could both get what we want?"

"You love Gristle, too?" Bridget gasped. "You'd better back off, girlfriend," she hissed at Poppy.

"No," Poppy said, shaking her head. "Bridget, no. That Troll that King Gristle put in his mouth? That's Creek. And I would do anything to save him. The problem is, we can't get anywhere near the king without him eating us!"

"Oh," Bridget said slowly, trying to understand what this little Troll was telling her.

"But *you* can!" Poppy continued. "You can walk

right up to him and tell him how you feel!"

Bridget snorted. "As if! I can't just walk right up to the king! His Royal Awesomeness would never talk to a scullery maid like me!"

Poppy smiled. "What if he didn't know you were a scullery maid? What if he thought you were this total babe?"

Bridget looked confused. "Huh? Why would he think that?"

Poppy exchanged a look with Satin and Chenille. The fashion-forward twins nodded, knowing exactly what Poppy had in mind.

CHAPTER
15

"**W**hat kind of total babe would be dressed like a scullery maid?" Bridget asked. "I smell like gravy."

Satin stepped forward. "What if we made you a new outfit? I'm thinking . . ."

". . . jumpsuit!" Satin and Chenille said at exactly the same time.

Bridget considered this, but she had her doubts. "What's the point of a jumping suit if I still have this?" She ran her fingers through her thin, limp hair.

"Oh, we can fix that," Poppy said confidently. All the Trolls nodded in agreement.

"What's the point of a new outfit and new hair if I don't even know what a total babe would ever say?" Bridget asked.

"We can help with that, too," Poppy said.

"Really?"

"What do you say, Bridget?" Poppy asked. "You get us Creek, and we'll get you a date with the king."

Bridget thought about it. Then she said uncertainly, "Um, let's do it?"

Poppy grinned. "A-five, six, seven, eight!" she said, cuing the Trolls.

"When you look in the mirror, let it disappear!" they sang. *"All your insecurities—"*

"Wait!" Bridget barked. The Trolls stopped.

Bridget pointed at Branch. "Why isn't this one singing?"

The Trolls turned to Branch and gave him their best pleading looks. "C'mon, Branch," Cooper said. "Sing with us!"

"Yeah, Branch!" Biggie agreed. "Sing with us!"

"Oh, no," Branch said. "That's okay."

The little bit of confidence Bridget had felt swiftly crumbled. "You don't think this will work?" she asked Branch.

He shifted uncomfortably from one foot to the other. "Oh, no. It's not that. I just don't sing."

"Branch . . . ," Poppy said, glaring at him. This was their one chance.

"No, he's right!" Bridget cried. "This idea's stupid. King Gristle will never love me!" She threw herself on her bed and started sobbing. The captured Trolls rushed over to console her, leaving Poppy alone with Branch.

"Branch, what are you doing?" Poppy whispered. "You have to sing."

"I told you," Branch said stubbornly. "I don't sing."

"Well, you have to."

"I'm sorry, I can't."

"No, you *can*," Poppy argued, getting annoyed. "You just won't."

"Fine," Branch said, equally annoyed. "I just won't."

"You have to!"

"No!"

"Why not?" Poppy asked in a harsh whisper. "Why won't you sing?"

"Because singing killed my grandma, okay?" Branch blurted. Horrible images flashed through his mind. "Now leave me alone."

The Trolls were stunned.

"My uncle broke his neck tap-dancing once," Cooper said, not very helpfully.

Poppy stared at Branch. "How did singing kill your grandma?"

Branch sighed. "*I* was the one singing. That day I was so lost in song, I didn't hear my grandma trying to warn me that a Bergen was coming. I just kept singing, really loudly. While my grandma tried to get my attention, the Bergen . . . took her. I never saw her again." Branch said he had been gray ever since that day. "And I haven't sung a note since."

CHAPTER
16

Poppy put her hand on Branch's shoulder. "I'm so sorry, Branch. I had no idea. I just assumed you had a terrible voice."

"No," he said wistfully. "It was like an angel's. At least, that's what Grandma used to say."

Poppy leaned in and gave him a big hug.

"Whoa, whoa," Branch said. "What are you doing? It's not Hug Time."

"I just thought you could use one," Poppy said.

Branch looked at her, touched. One by one, the other Trolls joined the hug. Bridget hugged all of them for a moment, until Branch wriggled free. "Hey, hey . . . no!" he said. "No, no! Okay, okay. I'll help. But I'm still not singing."

Everyone, including Bridget, seemed okay with the compromise. Poppy and the other Trolls started work on Bridget's new look. Satin and Chenille whipped up a stylish pink jumpsuit patterned with brown squares. They added a white belt, white platform shoes, and a hot-pink purse. Then the Trolls climbed onto Bridget's head and arranged their own long hair into a fabulous rainbow wig!

But more important than Bridget's new outfit was her new attitude: she was much more confident, self-assured . . . and happy!

She looked at herself in the mirror and squealed with delight. She was ready to strut her stuff, so they all headed out of the castle into Bergen Town, looking for King Gristle.

As Bridget glided along the sidewalk with the Trolls riding on her head, she looked down and spotted Barnabus, King Gristle's pet alligator. He was waiting outside while the king shopped inside a store called Bibbly Bibbington's Bibs.

Inside the shop, King Gristle was yelling at someone. "No, no, no!" he cried. "It's all wrong! I'm the king who is bringing back Trollstice! I need a bib to match!"

"Yes, sire," someone answered nervously. It was Bibbly Bibbington, the owner of the bib store.

Inside, King Gristle stood on a carpeted box in front of a mirror. Bibbly Bibbington knelt before him to measure the distance from the bottom of the king's bib to the floor.

King Gristle scowled. "I look like a child in this one," he growled.

"Oh, sire," Bibbington said, wanting to defend his bib but afraid to contradict the king.

"I need something elegant, sophisticated," King Gristle explained. "You know, a *man's* bib!"

Bibbly Bibbington sighed. He'd been bringing the king different bibs to try on for hours now. He was running out of bibs.

Outside, Bridget cautiously approached the store's window and peered inside. She spotted King Gristle standing on the box, frowning. He removed a green bib and handed it to Bibbly Bibbington.

"Oooh," Bridget sighed dreamily. "He's so beautiful."

Underneath her rainbow wig of Troll hair, Branch looked confused. *That* Bergen king? *Beautiful?* He really couldn't see it, but he supposed to a fellow

Bergen, maybe the king could somehow look attractive.

Poppy leaned over to Bridget's ear to give her a brief pep talk before she approached the king. "He's beautiful, and so are you!" she said.

But now that she was within moments of walking up to the king, Bridget began to lose her newfound confidence. "Oh, he'll know that I'm just a scullery maid!" she cried.

"No!" Poppy said. "No, he won't! Don't you see? Now that you're letting your true self come out, you'll seem like a completely different person to him!"

"My true self?" Bridget said, panicking. "In a rainbow wig made out of Trolls' hair? Ahh . . . I gotta get out of here!"

CHAPTER
17

Poppy spoke directly into Bridget's ear. "You've got this, Bridget. Don't worry. I'll be right here for you. We all will!"

Bridget took a deep breath. Then she stood up tall on her platform shoes, regaining her confidence. "You'll tell me what to say, right?"

"Of course I will," Poppy promised.

"Of course I will," Bridget echoed.

"Just, um, wait until we get inside," Poppy clarified.

In the store, Bibbington was about to show the king another bib. He'd been saving this one. If King Gristle didn't like it, he wasn't sure what he would do. Possibly quit the bib business forever.

"Oooh, sire," Bibbington gushed, "I believe we have the perfect bib!"

"It'd better be perfect!" King Gristle said in his most imperious voice. "Trollstice is tomorrow night!"

Bibbington stepped behind a cabinet, opened a drawer, and held up a glorious bib with a winged creature emblazoned on it. King Gristle stared at it, awestruck.

"Oh, wow," he said slowly. "It's got a wing-dingle on it."

"Would Your Majesty like to try it on?" Bibbington asked politely.

"Yes! Yes!" the king said, excited.

Bibbington stepped around the cabinet, carrying the bib. He carefully lifted it over the king's head and lowered it onto his chest. It fit perfectly.

The shop owner stepped back to admire the king. He clapped his hands in delight. "Oh, Your Majesty!" he exclaimed. "Look at you! Such a big, big boy!"

King Gristle practically ran across the store to examine himself in the mirror. He stared at his reflection and smiled. "I love it," he said.

The guards who had accompanied the king to Bibbly Bibbington's Bibs applauded.

But then a voice said, "I think you look PHAT."

Everyone gasped! The king was furious. Fuming, he sputtered, *"What?"*

He turned and spotted Bridget standing in the entryway of the store, a stunning vision in her pink jumpsuit and rainbow wig. Poppy leaned close to Bridget's ear and whispered, "P-H phat. Then strike that pose we worked on!"

"P-H phat," Bridget said, striking a beautiful pose.

King Gristle stood there in his new bib, staring. "Hot lunch!" he muttered. "Total honesty from a total babe!"

Inside Bridget's rainbow wig, Branch was confused again. *Really? Bridget? A total babe?* he thought. He decided he'd never be able to see a Bergen through another Bergen's eyes. *Thank goodness.*

Bridget giggled, and King Gristle practically floated across the shop to her. "And who might you be?" he asked, trying to sound as charming and suave as possible.

"Uh . . . eh . . . ," Bridget said weakly. She couldn't say her real name. What if he'd heard someone call her by that name in the castle?

In Bridget's wig, Poppy tried to think fast. Why

hadn't she thought of a new name for Bridget before? "Your name is . . . ," she said. But her mind went blank. "Uh . . . uh . . ."

The other Trolls jumped in, ready to help out.

"Uh, uh . . . Lady!" Biggie whispered.

"Glitter?" Guy Diamond suggested, naming something that was never far from his mind.

"Sparkles!" Smidge hissed, thinking of one of her favorite things.

"Seriously?" Branch whispered to Poppy. This was a disaster!

But Bridget didn't miss a beat. She told the king, "My name is Lady Glittersparkles. Seriously."

King Gristle didn't seem to think it was an unusual name at all. "Well, m'Lady Glittersparkles," he said. "Would you care to join me for an evening at Captain Starfunkle's Roller Rink and Arcade?"

Bridget's eyes widened, and so did her smile. "*Would* I?" she gasped. Then she turned her head aside and whispered to Poppy, "Would I?"

"Yes!" Poppy whispered. "You'd be delighted."

"Yes!" Bridget echoed. "You'd be delighted."

King Gristle grinned. "Oh, indeed I would!"

Inside Bridget's wig of Troll hair, Branch asked

Poppy, "When are you gonna ask him about Creek?"

"Well," Poppy said, "we have to warm him up first. Don't you know anything about romance?"

"Of course," Branch said. "I'm passionate about it."

"Really?" Poppy asked, amazed.

"Don't you know anything about sarcasm?" Branch asked her.

Meanwhile, King Gristle offered Lady Glittersparkles his arm as they walked out of the shop. "And I'll take one of everything, Bibbly," the king called as he left. "Things are gonna get *messy*."

King Gristle was right. The pepperoni pizza served by Captain Starfunkle was greasy, dripping sauce, and delicious. As the owner set the steaming pizza pie on the table in front of King Gristle and Lady Glittersparkles, he said, "Enjoy your pizza!" Then he dropped a handful of tokens on the table. "And the arcade games!"

Bridget smiled demurely and reached for a slice of pizza. "Oooh, so fancy!" she said. "Good thing I brought my appetite!"

The king reached for the same slice and their hands touched. Then . . . *whap!* Bridget slapped the king's hand away, grabbed the slice, and chowed down. King Gristle stared at her, completely enchanted.

"You are fantastic," he said.

Poppy whispered in Bridget's ear, "Compliment him back."

"I like your back," Lady Glittersparkles told the king.

"No," Poppy said. "I mean say something nice about him!"

"But I *do* like his back!" Bridget whispered.

"Heh?" King Gristle said, confused by Bridget's comment about his back.

Bridget stared, like a deer caught in headlights. "Um . . . uh . . . ," she said.

CHAPTER
18

"Quick, Poppy!" Branch said frantically. "Help her!"

Poppy tried to think of a good compliment. "Um, your eyes, uh, they're . . ." But she couldn't think of anything good to say about King Gristle's dry, beady little eyes.

"Ooh, your ears . . . ," Poppy said. What were his ears? Pointy? Looking like a bat's ears? *Argh!* Those didn't sound like compliments.

Bridget stared at the king, listening to Poppy's suggestions. He was waiting for her to explain herself. "Your eyes," Bridget said, "uh, your ears."

In the rainbow wig, the other Trolls jumped in with their suggestions on things to compliment.

"Neck!" Cooper said, thinking of his own most prominent feature. "Nose!" Biggie said.

"Skin!" Satin and Chenille said.

Overwhelmed, Bridget just mindlessly repeated everything the Trolls said. "Skin, neck, ears, nose, face, back of your head."

King Gristle looked concerned. Guy Diamond sang, "YOUR TEEEEEEETH," drawing out the word for emphasis.

"Your teeeeeeeth," Bridget dutifully repeated.

"What's going on?" King Gristle asked, frowning. "Are you making fun of me?"

Then Bridget, with a calm look on her face, said, "Your eyes. They're like two pools so deep, I fear if I dive in . . ."

Who said that? Poppy looked at the other Trolls. They shrugged. Who was whispering these poetic words of romance in Bridget's ear? Poppy couldn't believe it. It was Branch!

He continued, ". . . I might never come up for air."

". . . I might never come up for air," Bridget echoed.

In Bridget's wig, Poppy stared at Branch, who had his eyes closed. "And your smile," he went on. "The sun itself turns jealous and refuses to come out from behind the clouds . . ."

King Gristle stared at Bridget, stunned by the beautiful compliments.

". . . knowing it cannot shine half as bright," she said, smiling sweetly.

The king laughed awkwardly, showing his pointy, cracked, crooked Bergen teeth. "I kinda do have a nice smile, don't I?" he said bashfully.

Branch whispered a simple answer into Bridget's ear. "Yes, you do."

But Bridget didn't repeat what Branch whispered. Full of confidence, she suddenly spoke from her heart. Blushing, she said, "I can't believe I'm about to say this . . ."

In her wig, Biggie looked worried. "Guys, she's going rogue!"

". . . but being here with you today makes me realize that true happiness is possible," Bridget told the king. Poppy was impressed that Bridget was expressing her true feelings!

"It is," he said, smiling. "True happiness is a lot closer than you think." He scooted closer to Bridget in the booth. "It's right *here*."

Bridget thought the king was going to tap his heart, but instead he tapped the locket he wore around his neck. She was a little disappointed. "Oh, that's pretty," she said. "I guess."

"Wait'll you see what's *inside*," King Gristle said, opening the locket to reveal a sweaty, panting, and uncentered Troll. It was Creek, and he was alive!

Poppy and Branch gasped! "Creek!" Branch said, amazed.

"I *knew* he was alive!" Poppy exclaimed. The other Trolls let out a hushed cheer. Biggie hugged his pet worm. "Mr. Dinkles, he's alive!"

"Oh, snap!" said Mr. Dinkles in a deep voice.

The Trolls stared at Mr. Dinkles in shock. Biggie leaned down and looked into his pet worm's eyes, amazed. "You just talked!"

"Mew!" Mr. Dinkles mewed, as if nothing unusual had happened.

King Gristle held Creek between two fingers. "I've been savoring this little guy," he explained.

"HELP!" Creek screamed.

CHAPTER
19

King Gristle dropped Creek back into the locket and closed it. *Snap!* "Tell me, m'lady," he said to Bridget, "will I be seeing you at the Trollstice feast?"

"Well, duh," Bridget said absentmindedly. "I'll be working."

"It!" Poppy whispered in her ear.

"It!" Bridget echoed. "Working *it*. You know, workin' it!"

King Gristle grinned and nodded. "Yeah! You're not kidding, you will! 'Cause you're gonna be there as my plus-one."

Bridget beamed. "Really?"

"Assuming you'll say yes," King Gristle said.

"Yes!" Bridget blurted, not needing any prompting from Poppy or the other Trolls. She couldn't believe she'd be going to the Trollstice feast as the king's guest, or . . . (dare she think it?) date!

"Yes!" King Gristle shouted, pumping his fist.

"Yes!" said all the Trolls in Bridget's wig.

"In the meantime," King Gristle said, "maybe we should find some way to . . . work up an appetite." He held a pair of kneepads and opened their Velcro straps. *RRRRRIP!*

"Oh, yeah?" Lady Glittersparkles said. "What did you have in mind?"

Moments later, the two Bergens were joyfully roller-skating around the rink, moving in time to the music. The faster they skated, the tighter the Trolls had to hang on to keep from flying off Bridget's head.

King Gristle and Lady Glittersparkles linked arms, lifted hands, and locked ankles as they whipped around the rink. Lady Glittersparkles even held the delighted king over her head as she skated backward.

Bridget was thrilled. She'd never felt happier, more confident, more herself. She imagined that the two of them were soaring through outer space, rolling around a planet on its rings. As they leaned toward each other, about to share a kiss, one of the planets above them twirled around, revealing Chef's face!

"Your Majesty!" Chef barked.

The two skaters snapped out of their outer-space fantasy to see Chef glaring at them. "You seem to be having . . . fun," she sneered at the king.

"Oh, I am!" King Gristle said, enjoying himself way too much to notice the nasty tone in Chef's voice. "Meet the lovely Lady Glittersparkles!"

"Hmmm," Chef said, staring at Bridget, examining her closely. It was all Bridget could do to keep from trembling. Would Chef recognize her in the new outfit and rainbow wig?

"You remind me of someone," Chef said slowly.

Poppy, Branch, and the other Trolls held their breath.

Bridget was just about to confess and throw herself on their mercy when Chef said, "Wait a minute. Are you by any chance a descendant of Anton Glittersparklz? That's Glittersparklz with a *z*. How do *you* spell it?"

Poppy said quickly in Bridget's ear, "*S! S!*"

"*S! S!*" Lady Glittersparkles repeated.

Chef looked intrigued. Or possibly suspicious. "Two *s*'s? Interesting. . . ."

King Gristle looked at Lady Glittersparkles

adoringly. "She's gonna be my plus-one. At the Trollstice feast."

"Oh, wonderful," Chef said, relieved. "For a moment there, I was concerned that you were . . . changing the plan." Chef did *not* like having changes to her plans.

King Gristle chuckled. Lady Glittersparkles laughed nervously, still worried that Chef might recognize her as the scullery maid.

From inside the rainbow wig, Cooper joined in, laughing absentmindedly.

"Shhh! Cooper!" the other Trolls said. Luckily, the Bergens didn't hear.

"Well, your plus-one won't be a problem at all, Your Highness," Chef said agreeably. "I'll just tell my worthless scullery maid to get another place setting ready for the lovely Lady Glittersparkles with two *s*'s." She eyed Bridget suspiciously.

"Put her place setting next to mine," King Gristle ordered. "I want her right by my side." He turned to smile at Bridget . . .

. . . but she was gone!

CHAPTER 20

"Hey!" the king exclaimed. "Lady Glittersparkles?" He looked around for her, but saw only the front door to Captain Starfunkle's Roller Rink and Arcade standing wide open. Still wearing his skates, the king hurried outside.

A grand, sweeping staircase led down from the entrance to Captain Starfunkle's. "Lady Glittersparkles!" he called. Looking around, the king spotted Bridget's rainbow wig rounding a corner in the distance. "I'll see you at Trollstice, yeah?" he shouted after her, his voice full of hope and love.

He spotted something on the top step: one of Lady Glittersparkles's roller skates!

With a gasp of joy, the king bent over, picked up

the skate, and clutched it to his chest. "I miss you already," he said longingly. He spun the skate's wheel and gently kissed it . . . but burned his lips. "Ouch!" he yelped.

Back in the castle, Bridget zoomed through the halls, roller-skating on one leg and running on the other, still dressed in her jumpsuit and rainbow wig. She was worried someone would see her, but luckily, no one did. She'd left Captain Starfunkle's Roller Rink and Arcade so abruptly because she wanted to make sure she got back to the castle before Chef did.

When she reached her tiny room, she rushed in, closed the door behind her, and leaned against it. Then she threw herself on her bed. The Trolls tumbled off her head.

"I think the king really likes us!" Cooper said.

"I know, right?" Biggie said. They both stared off into space dreamily.

Bridget was ecstatic. "This was the greatest day of my life!" she squealed. "I'm so happy, I could just scream." She gave a tiny, quiet scream: *"Ahhhhh!"*

The Trolls started hugging each other in celebration. "I could scream, too!" Poppy exclaimed. "Creek is alive!"

She let out a delighted whoop. The other Trolls joined in. Then they all heard a frightening, bloodcurdling cry. *"Yaarhhhh!"* They all turned and stared at Branch.

"Branch, what's wrong?" Poppy asked, concerned.

"Nothing," Branch said, looking puzzled. "I thought we were celebrating."

"That's your happy shout?" Cooper asked.

"It's been a while," Branch admitted, embarrassed.

Poppy grinned. "Well, you're gonna have plenty of practice, 'cause we're gonna save Creek, and life will be all cupcakes and rainbows again!"

"Up top!" Branch said, holding his hand up for a high five. When Poppy raised her hand to slap it, he yanked his hand away. "Too slow." They shared a quick smile. Then Poppy got back to business.

"Okay, everybody!" she announced. "Let's go save Creek!" But as she led the Trolls toward the door, Bridget jumped up in a panic.

"No!" she cried. "You can't leave! Lady Glittersparkles is going to be the king's plus-one at dinner!"

Branch made a face. "The dinner where they're serving Troll? Yeah, I think we're gonna have to skip that one." They all started to leave.

"No, no! You have to help me be Lady Glittersparkles! I *need* you!" Bridget pleaded.

Poppy hesitated. She felt sorry for Bridget, but she wanted to hurry up and save Creek before King Gristle stopped savoring and started chomping. "You don't want to pretend to be someone you're not forever," she said.

"Then how about just for tomorrow?" Bridget asked reasonably.

Poppy took a step toward the scullery maid. "Bridget, remember when you spoke from your heart? That was amazing! You and King Gristle made each other happy. You don't need us anymore."

Bridge shook her head so violently, her pigtails smacked her cheeks. "No! Lady Glittersparkles made him happy. I don't know how to do that!" She ran to the wall, tore back the curtain, and started ripping down all the pictures of King Gristle.

"Bridget," Poppy said.

"Just go!" Bridget said, crying. "Get outta my room! Leave me alone!"

"Please listen."

"BRIDGET!" Chef screamed down through the

opening from the kitchen. "WHAT'S GOING ON DOWN THERE?"

Smack! A dirty dish fell down and landed right on Bridget's head, smearing food across her face.

"Bridget!" Chef bellowed. "Scrub that dish! The king's bringing a plus-one."

"Yes, Chef," Bridget whimpered up into the opening. She broke down, sobbing. Poppy watched, her heart going out to Bridget.

But they had to save Creek.

In his royal bedroom, King Gristle tossed his furry cape and the locket with Creek trapped inside onto his bed. He gently placed Lady Glittersparkles's skate next to it.

The king turned to his pet alligator. "We can do this, Barnabus! I just have to lose thirty pounds in the next eight hours!"

He put on a headband and a pair of headphones and hopped onto his treadmill. While he walked, he couldn't hear anything but loud music.

Poppy, Branch, and the other Trolls peeked in through the bedroom door. Cooper saw the locket and pointed it out to everyone.

"There it is!" Poppy said. "Good spotting, Cooper!"

They snuck across the room, climbed onto the bed, and made their way to the locket. Branch struggled to open it.

Poppy whispered, "Creek, we'll have you out of there in a second!"

"Hurry!" Biggie urged Branch. "It's stuck!" he said. Suddenly, a reflection appeared in the locket's polished green jewel.

Barnabus.

"Uh-oh," Branch said.

CHAPTER 21

"**R**UN!" Branch said, still yanking frantically on the locket's cover. He and Poppy picked up the locket and took off.

"*YAAAAAH!*" screamed the Trolls.

King Gristle continued to exercise, hearing only the music in his headphones. Barnabus chased the Trolls around the room, trashing it as he scrambled to catch them, snapping his jaws.

The king didn't even notice.

Poppy and the other Trolls sprinted to Lady Glittersparkles's roller skate, tossed the locket on it, and jumped on, launching the skate off the bed and into the hallway. Barnabus was right behind them.

Biggie cried, "Hold it steady!"

As they raced down the hallway, Poppy yelled, "Satin, Chenille! Sharp right!"

"Let's do it!" Chenille shouted.

Chenille flipped Satin onto the wall. The twins used their shared hair to slingshot the roller skate around a sharp corner. Barnabus skidded around the corner, too, hot on the trail of the Trolls.

"Guy Diamond!" Poppy yelled. "Glitter that gator!"

"YOU GOT IT!" Guy Diamond said, grinning. He climbed down the back of the skate and ground his glittery butt on the spinning wheel, kicking up a cloud of sparkling glitter exhaust. "EAT GLITTER!" he cried.

The glitter seemed to slow the big reptile down—a little—but unfortunately, the roller skate started to spin.

"Why are we spinning out of control?" Biggie wailed.

"That's why!" Poppy said, pointing at a sign that read CAUTION! WET FLOOR! The skate slammed right into the sign, rolling up it and flying out an open window at the end of the hall!

"HOLD ON!" Poppy shouted. The Trolls gripped the sides of the skate, but the locket with Creek inside bounced out of the skate and right into Barnabus's mouth!

"Creek!" Poppy called.

Choking on the locket, Barnabus slid into the windowsill. *Wham!* He spat out the locket. Poppy jumped out of the skate to catch it midair. "Branch!" she shouted.

She whipped her hair back to Branch. He whipped his hair to catch Poppy's hair and yank her back into the skate.

"We've got you!" Biggie called.

Still flying through the air, the skate with the Trolls on it crashed through a window—*SMASH!*—into another part of the castle. *"AAAAHHH!"* they screamed.

Riding the skate, the Trolls smashed through a lamp, a chandelier, a china cabinet, and a marble bust of King Gristle until they finally landed in a heap in the kitchen.

Poppy stood up and shook off the rough landing. She noticed that the locket had opened in the crash. "Creek!" she cried. "We'll have you out of there in a second!"

The Trolls rushed to the locket—only to find that

it was empty! That could only mean—

"No," Poppy said. "He can't be gone."

"I'm sorry," Branch said. "We're too late."

Poppy's eyes filled with tears. Without even thinking, Branch reached out to hug her.

"Actually," Chef said, "your timing is perfect." *WHAM!* She slammed a cage down over Poppy, Branch, and the other Trolls.

Biggie grabbed the bars of the cage and began to cry. "I don't like it! I don't like it!"

"Sorry," Chef sneered, "but I can't have you leaving before tomorrow's dinner. A dinner to which you're all invited! And when I say all, I mean *every* Troll in Troll Village."

"You'll never find them," Poppy said defiantly. "Not where they're hiding."

"Oh, you're right," Chef admitted. "*I* couldn't find them. By myself. But I could with someone they know. Someone they trust. Someone . . ."

She took something out of her leather pouch. It was Creek!

". . . like this guy," she said.

"Creek?" Poppy exclaimed. "You're alive!"

"He's selling us out!" Branch yelled. He whipped his long hair at Creek, but Poppy pulled him back.

"Branch, wait!" Poppy said. "I'm sure there's a reasonable explanation. At least give him a chance."

"Thank you, Poppy," Creek said gratefully. He paused, took a deep breath, and said matter-of-factly, "I'm selling you out."

This time it was Poppy who whipped her hair out between the bars of the cage at Creek. The other Trolls grabbed Poppy, struggling to pull her back. "No! Leave him alone!" they cried.

Poppy released the grip of her hair from around Creek's throat. "You'd better explain yourself, Creek," she demanded.

Rubbing his throat and catching his breath, Creek said, "It *will* make sense, I promise. As I was about to accept my fate, quite nobly, I had what I can only describe as a spiritual awakening."

CHAPTER 22

Creek told his former friends the story of how he had come to betray them.

"I DON'T WANT TO DIE!" he had screamed when King Gristle was about to eat him. In that moment, he realized he would do anything to save himself. He was just too groovy to die young, so he had agreed to show Chef where all the other Trolls were hiding.

To keep from being eaten, he was going to lead Chef back to the Troll Village and lure the Trolls into her grasp.

Poppy was shocked. "Creek, you can't do this."

"Believe me," Creek said, "I wish there were some other way—"

"But there isn't," Chef said, sharpening a long knife.

Creek stepped slowly toward the cage. "And now I have to live with this for the rest of my life. At least you get to die with a clear conscience. So in a way, you *could* say I'm doing this for you." He reached through the bars and took Poppy's cowbell out of her hair. Then he gently touched her nose and said, "Boop."

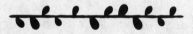

Chef took Creek back to the Troll Village and set him down in the middle of the town square. He raised Poppy's cowbell over his head and started to play it.

In Branch's underground bunker, King Peppy heard it. "Shhhh," he said. "Listen! It's Poppy's cowbell! She did it!"

Cheering, the Trolls all rushed out of the bunker expecting to see their princess. Instead, they saw Creek, sitting in the lotus position. He began to float in the air. They couldn't see that Chef was lifting him by his hair. And by the time they could, it was too late.

"Uh-oh," King Peppy said. "RUN!"

Chef and her guards quickly gathered up the Trolls and headed back to Bergen Town.

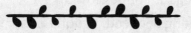

Trollstice had finally arrived. Bergens flocked to the castle, chanting, "Trollstice! Trollstice! Trollstice!" A huge banner hanging over the front door read HAPPY TROLLSTICE!

King Gristle stood outside the banquet hall holding Lady Glittersparkles's skate, scanning the crowd, looking for his plus-one. He had never felt so giddy before.

In the kitchen, Chef walked toward a huge pot carrying a sack squirming with Trolls. "Now let's prepare the main course," she said. She lifted the lid off the pot and laughed maniacally as she upended the sack over it. All the Trolls fell into the pot. Branch helped King Peppy to his feet.

"Poppy?" the king asked, looking around for his daughter. "Are you okay?"

Poppy looked at all the trapped Trolls. "Oh, yeah," she said. "Doing great. I got everybody I love thrown into a pot."

Biggie gasped, "Poppy, are you being . . . sarcastic?"

"Yes!" Poppy snapped.

The Trolls gasped!

"Oh my gah," Smidge said.

Poppy hung her head. "I don't know why I thought I could do this. I don't know why I thought I could save you. Looking on the bright side all the time just makes you blind."

Branch hung his head, too. It gave him no pleasure at all to hear Poppy talking the way *he* had during their journey together to Bergen Town.

Poppy looked him in the eye. "You were right, Branch. You were right about me." She turned to her father, defeated. "I'm sorry, Dad. I let you down. I let everybody down."

King Peppy looked at her with love and empathy. Being a leader was never an easy responsibility.

"But, Poppy—" Branch said.

She knelt to the ground and cut him off. "Face it, Branch. We're all going to be eaten." She had never felt so hopeless. The color began to drain from her.

In just a few seconds, Poppy turned completely gray. For the first time in her life, Poppy had lost all hope—and all of her pink color. Shocked, the Trolls stared at her. Without hope and fun and happiness, their color began to fade, too.

In her room, Bridget stared at her reflection in a dirty dish. She glanced at her bed, looking longingly at her Lady Glittersparkles jumpsuit and her one remaining roller skate. Tears ran down her cheeks as she washed the dishes for the feast.

In the banquet hall, King Gristle sat in his seat at the head of the long table, still watching for Lady Glittersparkles's arrival. But no more guests arrived. He pulled out the single roller skate and stared at it.

Inside the big pot, all the Trolls had become completely gray. Poppy looked utterly lost.

Then, unexpectedly, a voice started singing. . . .

The voice was sweet and clear, like an angel's.

The Trolls looked around to see where this angelic voice was coming from. A dream? The sky? Heaven?

No. It was Branch.

The Trolls were astonished. Branch *never* sang! Never.

But he was singing now. He sang a gentle song about how it was easy to lose your courage when the world turned dark. And about how small you could feel in a big, cold world. As he sang, he knelt by the gray princess, taking her chin in her hand and raising her face to look up at him.

Poppy's Hug Time watch opened and chimed. Branch opened his arms, offering her a hug, but she turned away.

One by one, the other Trolls' Hug Time watches chimed, too, until all the watches were playing the tune to the song Branch was singing.

Outside the cooking pot, Bridget listened sadly to Branch's song through a small hole in the lid. She'd reported to the kitchen for duty wearing her old scullery maid uniform.

WHACK! Chef hit Bridget on the head with a wooden spoon. Bridget gasped.

"What are you doing?" Chef barked. "The king is waiting! Get those Trolls up there!"

"Sorry, Chef," Bridget apologized.

"Oh, you *are* sorry," Chef sneered.

Inside the pot, Branch was still singing to Poppy. To him, nothing else mattered. He sang to Poppy with all his heart. He took her by both hands and got her to her feet. He sang to her about smiling and laughing. And he told her, in his song, that if the world made her crazy, she should just call him up, because he would always be there for her.

Then something amazing happened.

Starting with Poppy's toes, her pink color began to return. First her feet, then her legs, and soon her whole body—right up through the tips of her long hair—got all its color back!

"I see your true colors," Branch sang happily. *"And that's why I love you."*

Poppy looked surprised. She was amazed to hear Branch sing that he loved her. She began to sing with him. *"So don't be afraid to let them show. . . ."*

Poppy looked up into Branch's eyes. Touched by his open display of emotion, she reached out and took his hand . . .

. . . and something even *more* amazing happened.

Branch's gray hand turned a beautiful shade of green! The rest of his body turned green, too, and his hair a deep blue.

These were his true colors.

Branch and Poppy sang and danced together, and as they danced past the other Trolls, their vibrant colors came back. Now the Trolls all showed their true colors!

"Thank you," Poppy said.

"No, thank *you,*" Branch said.

"For what?" Poppy asked, confused.

"For showing me how to be happy."

"Really? You're finally happy? *Now?*"

Branch knew it didn't make much sense to be happy when they were trapped in a pot, about to be served to a bunch of hungry Bergens. "I know," he said. "But you were right—happiness *is in me.* And you helped me find it."

"You helped all of us," Biggie told Poppy.

Poppy smiled at her friends. "And just when I thought I didn't have it anymore, you guys gave it back to me."

"What do we do now?" Cooper asked.

That was a good question. All the Trolls, including Branch, looked to their leader, Poppy. She squared her shoulders. When her color had come back, so had her confidence. "I don't know," she admitted, "but there's always a bright side!"

Suddenly, it brightened inside the pot! Someone was lifting the lid, letting light stream in. The Trolls looked up and saw Bridget leaning over, peering in.

"Poppy," she said. "You've got to go."

Looking past Bridget's head, the Trolls saw stars in the sky. They weren't in the kitchen, or the banquet hall, or even the castle! Bridget had carried the pot outside!

"Bridget, what are you doing?" Poppy asked.

"I can't let them eat you," Bridget said simply. "C'mon, hurry! Go! Go! Go!" Using a ladle, she scooped the Trolls out of the pot and set them on the ground.

"No!" Poppy cried. "We can't just leave. If you go in there without us, they'll—" Poppy paused. She wasn't sure exactly what the Bergens would do to someone who'd helped the Trolls escape, but she was certain it wouldn't be nice.

"I don't care," Bridget said. "I'm just a Bergen. We're not meant to be happy."

Poppy shook her head. "Bridget, you're not just a Bergen. You're brave, and beautiful, and you're my friend."

Bridget's eyes got wide. "I think you're my friend, too. At least I got one perfect day, and it was all because of you."

From inside the castle came the sound of Bergens chanting, "Trolls! Trolls! Trolls! Trolls!"

"They won't wait much longer," Bridget said urgently. "Go on now. You have to hurry!"

Poppy got an idea. "Come with us!"

"And make it easier for them to find you? No way. You have to go. Now!"

Bridget stepped back inside the castle door and started to close it, but Poppy ran over to her, crying, "Bridget!" She hugged the Bergen's thumb.

Bridget let Poppy stay there for a second, but then she gently placed Poppy on the other side of the doorway. "Goodbye, Poppy," she said, closing the heavy door.

CHAPTER
23

In the banquet hall, the Bergens cheered when they saw Bridget nervously rolling a cart with a big pot on it. But King Gristle was still looking around the room anxiously.

"Chef," he said, "shouldn't we wait for Lady Glittersparkles?"

"Oh, you are absolutely right," Chef agreed. She turned to the hall and announced, "There will be no Trolls until the king's plus-one has arrived."

The crowd grumbled and booed.

"Unless," Chef said to the king, "she doesn't come at all. But that's crazy talk. Who wouldn't want to be with you?"

The king stared unhappily at the roller skate he

held in his hands. "Yeah," he said sadly. "Maybe we should start."

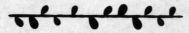

In the dark tunnels below the Troll Tree, the Trolls ran toward safety. "Go!" Poppy urged. "No Troll left behind!" But then she stopped and thought . . .

. . . and started running back the other way!

"Poppy?" King Peppy said asked as his daughter ran past him.

Branch spotted Poppy heading toward Bergen Town. He turned around and ran after her. When he caught up, he said, "Poppy, where are you going? What are you doing?"

"Bridget just ruined her life to save mine," Poppy said. "It's not right. She deserves to be happy as much as we do." She realized something. "They *all* do!"

She took off running again. "No Troll left behind? No *nobody* left behind!"

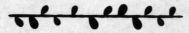

In the banquet hall, again the Bergens were chanting, "Trolls! Trolls!"

Chef addressed them. "All right, everyone! Let's get HAPPY!"

They all cheered.

Chef turned to the king. "King Gristle," she said, "there is only one thing that will ever make you happy. And only one Bergen who can provide it. *Bon appétit!*" With a flourish, she whisked the lid off the big pot.

It was empty.

"They're gone!" Chef cried.

"Gone?" King Gristle said.

Chef wheeled on Bridget. "Idget, what did you do? You ate them, didn't you? You greedy—!"

"N-no," Bridget stammered, backing away. "I—"

"BOOOO!" the crowd jeered. "SHE RUINED TROLLSTICE!"

"Guards," Chef commanded, "lock her up!"

The guards lowered their spears and moved toward Bridget, and then suddenly—

WHAM! Riding on the roller skate, the Trolls crashed into the banquet hall. They zoomed up Barnabus's tail, using it as a ramp to launch them into the air. They bailed from the skate and landed on Bridget's head, forming their hair into Lady

Glittersparkles's rainbow wig.

King Gristle hurried over to his plus-one. "Lady Glittersparkles!"

"What?" Chef exclaimed, astonished.

"But how?" the king asked, bewildered. "Why? Why did you do this?"

From her place in the wig, Poppy popped up. "Because she didn't think you would *ever* want a scullery maid like her!"

Bridget sadly removed the Trolls from her hair. "I mean, *hello*? Is it me you're looking for? I don't think so."

"Guards!" Chef ordered. "FINISH HER!"

As the guards moved in, Poppy turned to the king. "Wait! King Gristle, when you were with Bridget, you were feeling something, weren't you?"

King Gristle thought hard, remembering. "Yeah, I just thought it was too much pizza."

"Me too!" Bridget said. They stared at each other, reconnecting.

"That feeling?" Poppy said. "That was happiness."

All the Bergens gasped.

"But you have to eat a Troll to be happy!" Bibbly Bibbington said. "Everyone knows that! Don't you?"

The Bergens mumbled to each other, not sure of the answer.

But Poppy was. "No, you don't," she said firmly.

"Oh my gah," said a deep-voiced Bergen.

"Oh my gah!" echoed Smidge.

"King Gristle has never eaten a Troll in his life, right?" Poppy said, pressing on.

"And yet here I am," the king said, the truth dawning on him. He knelt in front of Bridget. "My belly empty, and my heart full."

"Awww . . . ," said the Trolls.

The king took out the roller skate Bridget had left behind and slipped it on her foot. The two smiled at each other. All the other Bergens watched, amazed. "They *do* look different," a Bergen remarked.

"Yes!" Poppy agreed. "Because they're *happy*! And each and every one of you can have the same."

"By putting a Troll in your mouth and chewing!" Chef shouted. "Don't you see? Only *I* can make you happy! *ME!*"

"No!" Poppy said. "She can't make you happy, and neither can I. Only *you* can make you happy. It's something that's already inside you, and it always has been."

She began to sing a happy song about feeling music inside you and dancing. Branch and the other Trolls joined in. And before they knew it, an amazing thing happened—the Bergens started singing and dancing, too!

Chef tried to stop them, but the Trolls tripped her with their hair. She fell onto the cart, landing right in the big pot. The cart rolled out of the banquet hall, down a hill, and out of town, taking Chef with it.

Thanks to the Trolls and their music, an absolutely incredible thing had happened: the Bergens, the most miserable creatures in the land, were happy!

CHAPTER 24

And so the Troll Tree came back to life, and the happy forest was once again filled with the happiest creatures the world has ever known: the Trolls . . . and the Bergens!

Putting the finishing touches on a scrapbook of his own, Branch said, "And because Poppy never gave up hope, she was able to do something that no one had ever done—unite the Bergens and the Trolls, and make *everyone* happy and safe. That's why she was going to be the best queen ever."

Poppy admired his scrapbook. "You scrapbook just as good as you sing!"

Branch spun his scrapbooking scissors around one finger. "I learned from the best. Check *this* out!" He opened the last page of the scrapbook. "YOU DID

IT!" cried a joyful voice as glitter shot out, covering Poppy.

"Perfect amount of glitter," she said, smiling.

King Peppy walked up to them. "Are you ready, Poppy?"

"Yes!" she answered, not a trace of doubt in her voice. She put on a long green cape and wove matching flowers into her hair.

The Trolls held a huge celebration for Poppy's coronation as queen. King Peppy proudly passed her the Torch of Freedom as music played and fireworks shot into the sky. To Poppy's delight, Branch sang in her honor.

"Our new queen!" King Peppy announced, presenting Poppy to the crowd.

And everyone lived happily ever after . . .

. . . except Creek. He now lived in the woods with Chef. She used his Troll hair to clean her pots and pans. It wasn't the grooviest existence, but it was still better than being eaten—plus being used as a scrub brush gave him plenty of time to practice his meditation.

"Om . . . omm . . . ommm . . ."